Loving You Always

Loving You Always

KENNEDY RYAN

New York Boston

Copyright © 2014 by Katennia Dula
Excerpt from *Be Mine Forever* copyright © 2014 by Katennia Dula
Cover design by Elizabeth Turner
Cover copyright © 2014 by Hachette Book Group, Inc.

Forever Yours
Hachette Book Group
1290 Avenue of the Americas
New York, NY 10104
hachettebookgroup.com
twitter.com/foreverromance

First published as an ebook and as a print on demand: October 2014

Forever Yours is an imprint of Grand Central Publishing.
The Forever Yours name and logo are trademarks of Hachette Book Group, Inc.

The publisher is not responsible for websites (or their content) that are not owned by the publisher.

The Hachette Speakers Bureau provides a wide range of authors for speaking events. To find out more, go to www.hachettespeakersbureau.com or call (866) 376-6591.

ISBN: 978-1-4555-5686-1 (ebook edition)
ISBN: 978-1-4555-5684-7 (print on demand edition)

Acknowledgments

I hope thank-yous are as hard for other writers as they are for me because maybe that means they have as many people to be grateful for as I do. I know I'll leave someone out, but the essentials are my husband and my son, who put up with the days when I forget that dinner is on me, and there is "real life" outside of the stories I write. You both drive me crazy and keep me sane as only those you truly love can do.

There are several bloggers I'd like to thank for supporting me in various ways. Megan from *Reading Books Like a Boss* and Christine Estevez from *Shh Mom's Reading*, who both have been so incredibly constructive and encouraging during this process, a delicate balance some aren't sure how to achieve. To Court and Shelley from *Must Read Books or Die* for buying into me and always looking for ways to support me. That truly means a lot. To Margie from *BestSellers & BestStellars* for loving my books and always, always, always making me feel like I should hang in there on days when I may have quit too soon. To Claire Contreras for helping me right in the midst of a difficult season for you. You helped me figure some huge things out here, and all while you had much more pressing things needing your attention. I hope I can be that gracious and selfless when new writers ask for my help.

To Latoya Smith, my editor for this book and the first, *When You Are Mine*. I will never, ever, ever forget that you took a chance on me, a complete novice and neophyte who asked dumb questions and stumbled through my debut. Your insight, instincts, and authenticity have impacted me as a writer, and I truly appreciate all you have done, and count you a friend.

To all the readers who truly LOVED my first book and reached out to me on Facebook, Twitter, email—thank you. It was not an easy book. The characters didn't make easy decisions, and it was hard for a lot of people, which makes you that much more special to me. I can't thank you enough for "getting" me and for wanting this story as much as I wanted to share it.

And to all my writer friends who are on this journey with me. I mentioned you in the first book, and I've added more folks since. And by the time this book comes out, there will be even more writers who have helped me along the way, because that is the kind of generous community I am so honored to be a part of.

Loving You Always

Chapter One

Walsh Bennett scowled at the teetering tower of paperwork overwhelming his desk.

"Trish, last time I checked we were in the twenty-first century," he yelled through the open door connecting his office to his assistant's. "What's up with all this paper? Nineteen ninety called and wants its dead trees back."

Trisha snickered and sauntered into his office, her matte red smile a vibrant slash in her golden brown face. She gestured to the offending paper pile, one hand on her curvy hip.

"The board expects your John Hancock on all these dead trees, so I hope 1990 sent pens."

Walsh grinned, shaking his head before obediently plowing through the documents requiring his signature.

"Do we still have coffee around here?" He tried to keep a straight face while he growled, but it hadn't taken Trish long to figure out he wasn't the slave driver everyone expected Martin Bennett's son to be.

"Would you like coffee, Walsh?" Voice saccharine sweet, Trish arched her brows at him, one of the little tricks she used to remind him that he might be the boss, but she wasn't his gofer.

"Why, yes, Trish. Now that you mention it, a cup of coffee would be delightful."

"Make him fetch it himself."

They both looked to the open door, where his cousin Jo Walsh stood like a queen paying a royal visit. Her chestnut hair waved in an angled bob past her shoulders, a studied, tousled, beautiful mess. Her black leather and tweed panel dress may as well have been poured over Jo's long, elegant body, its lines liquid against every firm curve. She strode deeper into the office, tossing her clutch onto Walsh's desk and lowering herself inch by inch into the seat facing him.

"Jo, to what do I owe this pleasure?" He looked away long enough to catch Trish's eye and send her on her way. "Coffee."

"I'm here for Fashion Week." She pointed to the dress. "Zac Posen show this afternoon. Donna Karan later."

"Ah, I'd forgotten that was this week. Moneyed fashionistas descending on New York City. One of your favorite times of the year."

When she remained silent, he looked up from the paper he was reading over before signing.

"Right? Don't you usually waste obscene amounts of money and spend the week hobnobbing with all the other wealthy women who just have to have this season's whatever? You and Mom always…"

Walsh let his words peter out, dropping the pen to give his

cousin his full attention. He looked past the glistening surface; he looked at her eyes beneath the smoky eye shadow and mascaraed lashes and saw grief, a twin to his own.

He and his father had spent the last month since his mother's funeral conducting business in Hong Kong. It had distracted him from the yawning hole in his heart, but every time he stopped for even a minute, the wailing monster inside reminded him his mother was gone. She would never return.

"It's my first Fashion Week without her." Jo straightened out the wobble in her voice before continuing, fixing her eyes on the large hourglass his father had given him, in its place of pride on his desk. "I know it seems flighty to you, but fashion was our thing. One of our many things. Doing this without her feels empty and foolish, but not doing it—"

"She'd want you to." Walsh stood and crossed around his desk, settled on the edge, and reached for Jo's hand. "Enjoy it as much as you can. We've gotta find joy wherever possible. Dad and I used work to survive the last month. You can certainly use fashion."

Jo ran the tips of her dark, square nails over a leather patch on her dress before looking back up at him.

"I miss you, cuz."

Damn. He had to add "asshole" to whatever titles his father and the board of directors wanted to bestow on him. How could he have neglected Jo? Sure, things had been strained between them before his mother had passed. All the drama with Kerris and Cam had managed to slither into his relationship with Jo, but she had needed him. Hell, he had needed her, and neither of them had reached for the other. Until now. He'd castigate himself as a self-centered so-and-so later. Right now he needed to fix this.

"Jo, I'm sorry we've barely talked. I didn't mean to abandon you. There was too much in Rivermont I needed to get away from. Mom's funeral and…"

Walsh didn't need to finish that sentence. Jo had stood witness to the Pompeii-like destruction of the scene with Kerris and Cam at their cottage. One kiss. It had leveled his friendship with Cam like a city, standing strong one minute, and nothing but rubble and ash the next.

Too many emotions tangled in his chest, a toxic helix of grief and regret and frustration. He missed his mother. He missed Jo. He missed Cam.

He missed Kerris.

In a matter of months, his closest relationships had disintegrated. If it hadn't been for his father—irony acknowledged—he would probably have been drowning in one-night stands, vodka, and his own vomit. In the past, tough times had coaxed out his darkest side like a serpent from a basket, snake-charming him into a mire of bad decisions. Not this time. The last two years had changed him. How could they not have? Meeting Kerris. Falling in love with her. Alienating Cam. And to some degree, Jo. Losing his mother. Building a relationship with his father. And he'd experienced most of it without the close friendship that had always anchored him.

"How's Cam?"

Walsh stroked his Hermès Pele Mele tie between two fingers, training his eyes on the subdued blue pattern instead of looking at Jo. She let him stew in that silence until he finally looked at her. A wile she'd learned from his mother.

"He's okay." Jo crossed one long leg over the other, leaning one elbow on the back of the seat. "Like you. Like me. Managing the pain, I guess. The baby helps…"

Walsh narrowed his eyes against the glare of horror in Jo's gaze when she realized what she had let slip. Caution, too late, tightened Jo's lips.

"Ah, that awkward moment when you realize the woman I love is pregnant with my best friend's baby."

"You know about…"

"That Kerris is pregnant? Yeah, I know."

"And you're okay?"

A bitter imitation of a laugh spilled across Walsh's lips. His heartbeat quickened. Probably because of the hot poker slicing through it when he considered Kerris having Cam's baby.

"Do I have a choice?" He pulled himself out of his own ass long enough to note the sadness filling Jo's eyes. Separate from grief. Personal. "And you?"

"What about me?" Jo jerked a shade down over her pretty face, cording off her emotions beyond his reach.

"Do you still love Cam?"

He was a son of a bitch for asking her that, but they hadn't discussed her feelings for Cam since the eve of his wedding to Kerris. Inquiring minds wanted to know.

Jo raised her brows and sat up in her seat, scooting to the edge. She rested her elbows on the armrests and impaled him with the blaze of her silvery eyes.

"I don't poach."

Just a few words, but a recrimination. A condemnation. A judgment he deserved. He clenched his jaw around shame and guilt and the defiant words that still, after everything he'd promised himself he'd forget about Kerris, lay on the tip of his tongue. Their eyes and wills dueled across the small space separating them until Jo eased the haughty lines of her face into something softer. A distant cousin of sympathy.

"What do you want me to say, Walsh? Do I have feelings for Cam? Probably for the rest of my life, if the last fifteen years are anything to go by. Would I ever do anything about them?" She shook her head, but held his eyes steady. "No."

How he missed those absolutes. Those black and white certainties that didn't account for tornadic emotion sweeping through and ripping at your convictions until they were negotiable with the promise of the thing you wanted more than life itself. He didn't say that. He barely breathed, lest he reveal how shaky his foundations were even now when it came to Kerris. Having her. Taking her. Keeping her for himself.

After spending time with his father for the last month, one thing he'd realized was that he was more like him than he had ever suspected. They shared more than dark hair and green eyes. Like his father, a predator lay in wait inside of him, relishing the hunt and capture. That beast would possess, careless of the consequences. With that legacy living inside him, he wasn't sure he could ever be around Kerris and Cam again.

Jo stood up and settled beside him on the desk, pushing her shoulder into his.

"They're happy. I want you to be happy."

Walsh leaned his head against hers, reaching for her hand. Letting himself be soothed by the familiarity of the closeness they had always shared.

"Besides," Jo continued, looking up at him with her smart aleck grin. "This is much too *Dawson's Creek*. Do you *want* to be Pacey in this scenario?"

Walsh laughed outright, slipping his arm around her slim shoulders. How had he forgotten how Jo made him laugh?

Suddenly the laughter melted from her voice and her eyes.

"Don't be Pacey. Joey's not worth it."

"What do you have against Joey?"

"She could never make up her mind and jerked those poor guys around for years. I hate indecisive women."

"Don't hate her, Jo. Kerris, I mean. It's not her fault."

"Who should I blame?" Jo glanced at the rose gold ALOR strapped around her slim wrist and picked up her clutch. "We were fine before she showed up."

"No, they were fine before I showed up."

Even after Jo had gathered her things and headed off for her front-row runway seats, Walsh echoed that statement back to himself.

They were fine before he showed up. And they'd be fine without him.

* * *

"How ya feeling?" Kerris Mitchell settled onto the bench at the kitchen table beside her husband, Cam.

The month since the funeral had been just as hard as she had imagined it would be. Cam missed Kristeene terribly. How could he not? She had been like a mother to him. Kerris had done everything she could think of to soothe him and take his mind off the dull pain. Cam had been shocked and incredibly moved by Kristeene's generosity in her will, as Kerris had been. She had left Cam a small fortune in stocks, along with the Land Rover he'd always loved so much. She'd willed a significant portion of her wardrobe to Kerris for Déjà Vu, the high-end consignment shop she owned with her best friend, Meredith.

"How do I feel? Like the king of the world." Cam touched her stomach, his hand a warm weight through the silk of the kimono she wore after her shower.

Kerris smiled at how gentle and considerate Cam had been since she'd told him about the baby.

"I mean about Kristeene."

"It's like having the worst day and the best day of your life...on the same day." Cam pulled his dark brows together even as the corners of his mouth turned up. "Ms. Kris would be so happy for us. You're happy, right?"

"Of course." She leaned her shoulder into his. "This is what we've talked about since the beginning. A family of our own."

"And you don't...you don't regret anything?" A small storm brewed behind Cam's blue-gray eyes, but the hand resting on her stomach remained steady.

Kerris knew, of course, what he was asking; the image he couldn't shake. There were moments when her mind would, of its own volition, revisit that moment, too; when her guard would slip, and she would be in Walsh's arms again. Feel his touch. Smell him. Taste him.

"I don't regret anything." She placed one hand over his on her still-flat stomach and ran the other hand over the silky dark hair hanging past his ears. "I'm as excited about this baby as you are."

His eyes plumbed hers, looking for the truth. She hoped what he saw satisfied.

"I wonder how she'll look." Cam finally spoke, a goofy grin at odds with his handsome face.

Kerris wondered, too. Since there was no record of either of her parents, she had no idea which ethnicities had collided to create her ambiguous looks: amber eyes, dark, silky hair, and skin the color of pale honey. Cam knew his parentage, though it wasn't much of a lineage. His prostitute mother had been half black and half Hispanic. His father, a white man. Some random john. He was routinely mistaken for everything from Italian to Puerto Rican. With their mishmash of a gene pool, there was no use trying to peg their daughter.

Wait? Daughter?

"Did you say 'she'?" Kerris laughed and ran a fond hand over the unruly spill of Cam's hair. "You know something I don't?"

"I just always think of the baby as a girl. I'll be happy with whatever, though. Healthy is what's important, right?"

Kerris nodded and smiled. Cam kissed her before standing to his feet.

"I'll be late for work if I don't get outta here. Not that I'll be working there much longer."

"Cam, you have to be careful with that money Kristeene left you."

"I'm not staying in that shitty graphic design job when I have stock worth millions, baby."

"I get that, but you don't have it yet." She walked over, grabbing his hands between hers. "It's a huge estate that's incredibly complex, and it's still being settled, papers have to be executed. I think it's good. Gives you some time to really think about the best thing to do with the money."

"You know what I've always wanted to do." He leaned down to kiss her nose. "I want to paint. Sebastian—you remember Sebastian, right? You met him at Kristeene's birthday party the night we got engaged."

"I remember him." Kerris walked over to clear their breakfast dishes from the table. "Every time I've swung by his gallery, he's never there."

"Been in Paris." Cam threw his voice over his shoulder as he moved toward the office to grab his backpack and laptop. "He's back. He thinks I should take a year to study in Paris. He says I have a lot of raw talent, but I need it refined. I need to train and study."

"A year?" Kerris's hands froze over the sink waiting for their breakfast dishes. "What would we—you mean *live* in Paris for a year?"

"Yeah, babe. Think about it." Cam came up behind her at the sink to wrap his arms around her. "The three of us in Paris, where some of the greatest artists did their best work. I could study at the Sorbonne. If I apply now, I could be accepted in the next six months."

"Six months." Kerris turned to face him, her back against the sink. "I'm only six weeks pregnant. Déjà Vu is just getting off the ground. I want to have our baby here in the States with a doctor I trust, surrounded by our friends. Our life is here."

Cam's smile dissolved into a straight line.

"Working that dead end job isn't much of a life. This money from Kristeene is a godsend. It'll give me the freedom to pursue my dream."

"I've always been your biggest cheerleader, you know that." Kerris evened her tone and placed a calming palm against his chest. "I'm just saying the timing may be a little off. Maybe in another eighteen months or so?"

"Eighteen months." Cam stepped back and stalked over to lean against the granite countertop, facing her with arms folded across the muscles of his chest. "You expect me to stay in Rivermont for eighteen months when I'll have money in the bank to pursue my dreams?"

"And my dreams?" She deliberately quieted her voice, not wanting this to explode between them. "What about the things I want to do? The business I *just* started? The family we're *just* starting? Are you considering any of that?"

"You know, maybe I'm missing something." Cam leveled his creased brows, his face giving nothing away. "Maybe there's something else you want to stay in the States for. Or should I say *someone.*"

Kerris reached behind her to clutch the rim of the sink. She turned her back to him, rinsing out the dishes she had left there. The muscles of her back tightened under the unrelenting burn of Cam's stare. They hadn't spoken of that moment again since that first night, but she knew it was still between them. He was a wounded animal secretly nursing his hurt.

"Cam, do we need to talk about Walsh again? I always thought we should have. We can't sweep it under the rug and pretend it didn't happen."

"Oh, I know it happened." His voice frosted over with fresh bitterness like new snow. "Do you think I will ever forget seeing you in my best friend's arms?"

"I told you it was only a kiss," she whispered, knowing that he would hear it in the eerie silence surrounding them. "We got emotional talking about Haiti—"

"Don't give me that shit again!" His voice erupting into the quiet made her jump. "Do you think I don't see how Walsh looks at you?"

Kerris, the way my son looks at you is like a starved man. It's like he can't bring himself to look at anything else in the room.

Kristeene's words in the hospital room that last day before she went home for good drifted back to Kerris. It had been months, but it felt like yesterday. Kerris tunneled her hands into the dark hair on either side of her head before turning to look directly at her husband. She clasped her hands together over the tightly coiled dread in her belly.

"And how do I look at him?" She braved the question, refusing to even blink until he had answered; determined to be as honest as he would allow.

"Most of the time you don't, which I think says just as much as the way he eats you up every time he looks at you. The two of you—"

"There is no two of us!" The volume of her own voice surprised her, reverberating in the solitude of their cottage.

"I'm out." He didn't acknowledge her statement, unfolding from his deceptively indolent stance against the counter and leaving the kitchen. "I'm gonna be late for this job you want me to stay stuck in for the next eighteen months."

Kerris charged out after him into the living room, ignoring the gibe about his job.

"There is no two of us." She stopped to stand in front of him at the door. Cam turned to her, his face tight, eyes hard.

"You think I'm stupid, Kerris? Is that it? You think I don't know how you feel about him?"

"What do you want me to say?" The words heated up in her mouth and boiled over. "I've told you that I love you. That it was a mistake. I'm not going anywhere. We're having a baby together."

"But is that enough?" Emotion chipped away at the hardness in Cam's eyes until they were a little softer, a little sadder. "What if it isn't enough? Then what do we do?"

And there it was. The fear that had skulked around in her heart since Cam first approached her about marriage that night so long ago. That what she felt for him wouldn't satisfy. Would they have ended up here anyway, or had those few moments with Walsh cost her everything she'd thought would make her happy?

"I gotta go or I'll be late." Cam's eyes scanned her face, and Kerris wondered what he was searching for. She wondered if he found it. "Think about Paris, Ker. Maybe all we need is a fresh start somewhere new."

He leaned down to whisper something against her stomach; something she couldn't hear. Something between him and the child they had made. He looked up and hesitated before standing and dropping a kiss on her cheek. And then he walked away.

Chapter Two

Tell me again why we're registering at Walmart?" Kerris's best friend and business partner, Meredith, pulled into a spot in the crowded parking lot and rolled her eyes.

Kerris laughed, climbing out carefully, still unused to the additional pregnancy weight she'd gained over the last five months. Nearly seven months' pregnant in the dead heat of summer. She wouldn't recommend it.

"A lot of ladies coming in the shop want to buy things for the baby. I registered at all those froufrou places you chose." Kerris shared a grin with her friend and wiped at the sweat on her neck. "I want to register somewhere those ladies can afford, too."

"I guess that makes sense." Meredith gestured to Kerris's baby bump. "And we still don't know blue or pink, huh?"

"No. Cam and I want to be surprised."

"You've had a great pregnancy." Meredith smiled, the delicate bones of her face and exotic eyes giving away her Asian ancestry. "I know ladies who were sick the whole time, and who gained so much weight they were barely recognizable. Though I barely recognize *you* anymore with the short hair. Have you gotten used to it yet?"

Kerris reached up to touch the soft hair curling around her neck, falling just shy of her shoulders. She had cut it a few months ago to honor Iyani. The little girl from the Walsh Foundation's Kenyan orphanage had come to America battling a brain tumor. In life and after her death, Iyani had left an indelible impression on Kerris. Cutting and donating twenty inches of hair to Locks of Love was such a small thing, but Kerris had wanted to do it. Cam had gone with her, grinning and taking pictures for Facebook with his phone.

Kerris wondered which Cam would come home tonight. He vacillated from the delighted daddy-to-be to the wronged husband who couldn't quite manage to forgive or forget her transgression.

"I'm gonna grab a cart," Meredith said. "There's always something you need at Walmart."

Kerris was studying a display while she waited for Meredith when she noticed a woman just a few feet away, checking and highlighting receipts for customers exiting the store. Kerris's feet stuck to the floor. Goose bumps sprung up on her arms. The woman, though older, looked just like…

"Mama Jess?" Kerris asked, hesitant, hopeful, taking the few steps that brought her directly in front of the older woman.

Highlighter in hand and dark brown eyes sharpening in her still-smooth brown face, the woman studied Kerris. New lines framed those eyes, but the kindness Kerris had seen as a child was still there. She wore an I ♥ NY T-shirt over a denim skirt.

Kerris blinked a few times, uncertain. She hadn't seen Mama Jess since she was ten years old. Maybe her memory hadn't served her right. Maybe her heart had leaped ahead and imagined this stranger as the woman she had always considered the mother she'd never had.

"I'm s-sorry." Kerris stuttered, embarrassed. "I thought you were—"

"Kerris!" The woman cut off Kerris's stilted apology.

Kerris hurled herself at Mama Jess like a cannonball, wrapping her arms completely around the woman's neck. Strong arms encircled her, pressing between her shoulder blades and pulling her as close as her swollen middle would allow.

"I'm sorry," Kerris mumbled through her tears, pulling away. "I've gotten your shirt all wet."

"Think I did the same." Mama Jess laughed and wiped away her own tears. "As I live and breathe, I didn't think I'd ever see you again, Lil' Bit."

"I wanted to find you after…" Kerris trailed off.

The past rose up between them, tragic and awkward. Kerris's reluctant, jumbled testimony on the witness stand had sent this woman's brother to prison, where he had died. Because of her, Mama Jess had lost all of the foster children she'd loved so much, and was probably never allowed to foster again.

"I wanted to see you, too." Mama Jess didn't look away, her voice soft and sure. "But I couldn't. I always prayed we'd find each other again, though. And after all this time…well, God knows."

"Mary!" an impatient voice called from behind them.

A balding man, not much taller than Kerris, crossed to where they stood. His mud-brown button-down shirt strained across his paunch. Censure was all over his face and in the eyes behind his wire-frame glasses.

"It's peak time, not time for socializing, Mary."

Kerris narrowed her eyes at the unpleasant man. She exchanged a quick look with Mama Jess, ready to snap at him on her behalf.

"Yes, sir, Mr. Crawford." Mama Jess offered a pleasant smile. "Just some old friends."

"Reunions on your own time." He harrumphed his displeasure and walked back into the store.

"Heard of a Napoleon complex?" Mama Jess asked from the side of her mouth. "That's him. Tries to make up for in mouth what he ain't got in inches."

"Probably not just inches in height." Meredith parked her cart to the side and frowned at Crawford's departing back.

"Mer!" Kerris pressed the back of her hand to her mouth to hold back a laugh.

"Oh, she's probably right." Mama Jess offered a hearty laugh of her own. "Who's this?"

"My friend Meredith. Mer, this is…"

How should she describe this woman? There was so much she'd only ever told Walsh, and then later, Cam. She grappled with the proper way to address the woman after all this time.

"It's Mary Jessup, but you can call me Mama Jess."

"Nice to meet you," Meredith said, shaking hands.

"Well, you heard the man," Mama Jess said. "I need to get back to work."

"We can't just—couldn't we…I mean, when do you get off?" Kerris was desperate not to lose Mama Jess again now that they'd run into each other. "Maybe we could have dinner or something?"

"My shift ends in about"—Mama Jess glanced down at her watch—"'bout an hour."

"We're registering for the baby," Kerris said. "Let's meet back here in an hour. Come home with me for dinner."

Mama Jess's smile was as warm and wide as Kerris remembered. She grabbed Kerris's hand and squeezed.

"I'd love that, Lil' Bit." She stepped back to reach for a customer's receipt, highlighter poised. "In an hour."

Kerris had trouble focusing on the registry items. Meredith, of course, buzzed with questions about Mama Jess, which Kerris answered as honestly as she could, without revealing too much.

"So why'd you have to leave her house?" Meredith scanned an item, searching Kerris's face.

Kerris struggled to find words, glancing up and down the aisle to see if they were alone. Was she really about to do this? Share a secret she had guarded so closely, on aisle seven with the formula, wipes, and diapers?

"Her brother molested me." Kerris pushed the words past her cold lips.

The *thud thud* of her heart drowned out the bustling sounds of the store around them, and the world narrowed down to the shelf in front of her. She fixed her eyes on the bib she was scanning while she waited for Meredith's response. The silence was thick and deafening. It went on so long Kerris finally made herself look over her shoulder. Meredith's eyes were filled with tears, her tiny fist clenching and unclenching at her side, her lips pressed together.

"Oh, Ker." Meredith pulled her into an embrace that communicated all the things she couldn't seem to find words for.

Kerris closed her eyes, relishing the contact. There were no tears, though. TJ wouldn't get another tear from her. He wasn't worth it. Didn't deserve it.

"It's okay." She rubbed her own soft cap of curls against the hair Meredith had recently chopped off and dyed platinum blond. "I'm okay."

"You wait to tell me something like that in the middle of Walmart?" Meredith finally offered a small smile that did its best to lighten the moment.

"The worst part was losing Mama Jess. And now I've found her again. I can't tell you what it means to me."

Kerris glanced at her watch, eager to finish registering and get back to the mother she had lost. To the only mother she had ever known.

That night, Kerris and Mama Jess caught up, preparing dinner together and speaking frankly about what the last decade and a half had held for them. Mama Jess made the lasagna Kerris remembered so well, even after all these years. Kerris scribbled the recipe, slipping it under a magnet on her refrigerator. She tossed the salad and squeezed lemons for lemonade. She was taking garlic bread from the oven when Cam walked through the door.

"Hey, baby." He dropped a kiss on Kerris's baby bump and cast a speculative glance at Mama Jess. "Something smells good."

"Hey, sweetie." Kerris searched Cam's handsome face to see if it would tell her which husband had come home. "You remember me telling you about my foster mother Mama Jess?"

Cam's face screwed up a little, obviously searching his memory. "Which one?"

Kerris wondered how she should qualify Mama Jess.

"My favorite one," she settled for, returning the smile Mama Jess sent her way.

"Oh, yes. I remember." Cam aimed a smile loaded with his deadly charm at Mama Jess.

Mama Jess contemplated him with a small curve of her lips, her eyes slightly narrowed at the corners.

"Nice to meet you," Mama Jess said. "You taking care of my Lil' Bit?"

"Um, yeah," Cam answered after a heartbeat. "Of course."

"Baby, dinner's almost ready." Kerris reached up with a smile to smooth his hair back. "Why don't you go put your things down in the office and come on back in to eat?"

Cam walked back toward the office, and Mama Jess pulled the lasagna out of the oven.

"That's a pretty man you got there." She set the dish on the stovetop.

"Yeah, he is. He's so excited about the baby."

"Now you're how far along?" Mama Jess leaned a full hip against the counter.

"I'm twenty-eight weeks," Kerris said, rubbing her belly.

"Waddling, huh?"

"A little."

"Using the bathroom all night."

"Yes."

"Ankles swelling."

"Some." Kerris grinned and glanced down at her semipuffy ankles. "Sounds like you know of what you speak. Did you ever have any kids?"

Mama Jess's face clouded and her mouth turned down at both corners.

"Only fostering." She looked at Kerris and some of the sadness passed. "Kids like you."

Before Kerris had time to respond, Cam stepped back into the kitchen.

"I can't wait another minute." Cam rubbed his hands together. "Starving and ready to dig in."

Mama Jess looked at him, and her face softened the way all girls' did for Cam.

"Then let's eat."

Chapter Three

Y ou know that Bennett boy is on TV tonight," a customer said, leafing through a rack of sundresses Kerris had found at a Charleston yard sale.

Kerris's hands hovered over the display of hats she was straightening. She had no idea what the customer was talking about. Kerris had heard Walsh's name so little since the funeral, but that didn't mean she hadn't thought about him, because she had even when she didn't want to.

"You want those hats from the back, too, Lil' Bit?" Mama Jess asked from the door to the storage room, turning back at Kerris's affirmative nod and affectionate smile.

Kerris had wasted no time persuading Meredith they needed help at Déjà Vu. Getting Mama Jess out of Walmart and away from the tyrannical Bonaparte wannabe had been easy. Mama

Jess had brought new life to the shop over the last month. She'd brought new life to Kerris.

"You gonna watch?" Meredith repositioned a few scarves.

Kerris glanced up over the pile of hats with a clueless smile pasted on her mouth.

"Watch what?"

Meredith shot Kerris a knowing glance. "The *Pinnacle* interview."

"I don't know what you're talking about."

"You know. *Pinnacle*, the TV magazine that has the '30 Under 30 List' each year. Walsh made the list, and they're airing his interview tonight."

Mama Jess walked up to them with a small mountain of hats.

"Who's Walsh?"

The back of Kerris's neck tingled and sweat broke out on her palms. Mama Jess was as sharp-eyed as they came. Kerris had noticed the considering look on Mama Jess's face every time she saw Kerris and Cam together. Mama Jess knew something was amiss in their marriage, but hadn't asked about it…yet. That didn't mean she wouldn't.

Cam remained mercurial. Coming home one day cooing over her belly, kissing her sweetly, encouraging her to put her feet up and rest while he unpacked food he'd picked up on the way home. And then the next day he'd be curt, demanding, and withdrawn. It added a thin layer of anxiety over the concerns Kerris already had, but she didn't know what to do about it. She hadn't contacted Walsh, and he hadn't reached out to them. He really was staying out of their lives. It was the only way this marriage could work, but Cam couldn't seem to let that moment between Walsh and Kerris go. And if Kerris were completely honest, neither could she.

Mama Jess was still looking at Kerris, waiting for her answer.

"Walsh is just a friend of Cam's." Kerris took the hats from her.

"His best friend, isn't he?" The customer who'd originally mentioned the interview inquired from across the room.

Big ears.

"He hasn't been back to Rivermont since his mother passed, though," another well-meaning customer chimed in.

"His mother? Who was his mother?" Mama Jess asked.

"Um, Kristeene Bennett." Kerris started displaying the hats.

Who in Rivermont didn't know Kristeene Bennett? The community had memorialized the woman with park benches, hospital wings, cobblestones, a new street sign, and even a sandwich that bore her name.

"Isn't he the one who was kidnapped a while back?" Mama Jess asked.

Kerris only nodded. She didn't want to think about Walsh, and certainly didn't want to watch some stupid interview that screamed he had moved on and was doing just fine without her.

It was perverse. She knew that. She knew they should have no contact, and in spite of the miracle growing inside of her, in spite of her marriage being semi-intact, in spite of her thriving business and her growing passion for her river stone jewelry—she *missed* Walsh. So much. It was a private ache she rarely even acknowledged to herself.

"Yeah, that's Walsh." Meredith gave Kerris a sharp glance. "He and Cam grew up together."

Kerris couldn't be in this conversation a moment longer.

"Do you ladies mind if I knock off a little early?" She reached around to the small of her back, massaging a fake ache. "My back hurts and my ankles are swollen."

Mama Jess glanced at Kerris's slim ankles in her strappy sandals.

"Your ankles look fine to me."

"No, they're definitely puffy." Kerris grabbed her purse. "I think I just need to lie down."

"Of course, Lil' Bit." Mama Jess pushed Kerris's hair back from her face. "Go on home. Put your feet up. Have some of that lemonade I fixed when I came over last night. And there was some corn pudding and baked chicken left over. You go on home and rest."

Kerris ignored the twinge of guilt Mama Jess's consideration pricked inside her.

"Thanks, Mama Jess."

"Maybe you can even watch that interview tonight, too," Mama Jess said to Kerris's back as she headed to the door.

Kerris stiffened and glanced over her shoulder at Mama Jess with narrowed eyes. Mama Jess offered an innocent smile that reminded Kerris just who she was dealing with.

Fifteen minutes later, Kerris entered the cottage, drawing in an air-conditioned breath. She started a bath, padding to the kitchen to check Mama Jess's leftovers. Cam had been working late a lot, and Mama Jess was often her dinner companion.

She sank into the vanilla-scented bubbles, letting them creep around her bare neck and shoulders. She allowed herself thoughts of Walsh. He was a glass of wine in her bath; heady, intoxicating. A forbidden pleasure as she lay swollen with Cam's child; a guilty indulgence that could endanger the things she wanted most.

She looked at her belly poking through the suds, smiling even while she blinked back tears. She shouldn't feel lonely. She was surrounded by friends who loved her. Living with a husband who had once said he'd never let her go. With the baby she'd always dreamed about steadily blooming inside of her. Was she so hard to satisfy? Even now, her body responded to the thought of Walsh touching her.

She closed her eyes, her skin heating in the cooling bath. She fled the tub as if she were being chased. And maybe she was. Chased by the memory of his touch, of his concern, his understanding.

She dried off, slipping on her ancient red kimono, tying it loosely over her baby bump and leaving her feet bare. And then exhaustion caught up with her. Her swollen ankles might have been fictional, but the bone deep fatigue that seemed to characterize this last trimester was real.

She napped for two hours, not stirring once, and got up feeling more refreshed, running her fingers through the drying curls skimming her shoulders. She grabbed her plate of leftovers and headed toward the television. She didn't watch much TV, but she did know that *Pinnacle* came on in ten minutes. She pretended to watch the local news in the meantime, her heart beating like she was about to see Walsh in person. Like an eclipse of moths had been let loose in her belly, and their madly flapping wings feathered her insides. She sat through the *Pinnacle* title package and the lead up. There were actually five others being featured tonight, and they saved Walsh for last.

"When we first took notice of this guy," the pretty, polished interviewer said, "he was Sofie Baston's plus one. Of course, he is handsome and comes from a prominent family, and is following in his father's business footsteps, but what intrigues us about him is his big heart. We sat down with the confirmed bachelor who has captured our imagination over the last few years. I'm sure it'll be clear to everyone why Walsh Bennett is on our '30 Under 30 List.'"

During her introduction, they cut to b-roll of Walsh walking a red carpet with Sofie, playing soccer with a group of children in Kenya, and blocking a camera's view as he left the church after Kristeene's funeral. Finally it cut to Walsh sitting down with the interviewer in what looked like a tropical location. A small, if guarded, smile played around his full mouth. His high cheekbones seemed more prominent than the last time she'd seen him. He'd lost some weight, but his tanned skin still stretched beautifully across the bones of his face. The smooth dark brows slashed over the penetrating green eyes. He wore a white polo shirt over his usual shabby designer cargo shorts.

"It's been quite a year, huh?" The interviewer's name, Shelby Jennings, flashed on-screen.

"Yep." Walsh's smile was no help, as if he wanted her to know she would have to work for this.

"I mean, kidnapped in Haiti and then a heroic rescue engineered by your father."

"You make it sound so dramatic." Walsh accompanied his sardonic tone with an equally sardonic smile.

"Well, your family is very prominent in this country, and for a few days we didn't know if you were dead or alive. The world was transfixed."

Walsh's smile died a quick death.

"No, a small portion of the world was transfixed. Most of the world was worried about finding clean water to drink and food to eat."

Shelby's hollow laugh showed some of her discomfort with Walsh's serious response.

"Well, you know what I mean." She laughed again, her second laugh as forced as the first. "Speaking of your family, we were all sorry to hear about your mother's passing."

Walsh acknowledged the canned condolence with a quick nod, his features not even tweaking with the pain Kerris knew must still lay just beneath the surface.

"She was a remarkable woman. She did so much for orphans all over the world." Shelby's face creased with just the right amount of sympathy and respect. "Your father is a titan in the business world. Is it hard to balance the business side of your life with your philanthropic interests?"

"Not at all. It's how I grew up. Working in acquisitions with my father is like an adrenaline rush for me. And serving with my family's foundation makes me feel like I'm part of something bigger than myself. I enjoy both."

"Now, you were dating Sofie Baston not too long ago, and then it seemed to end abruptly."

Shelby quieted, obviously hoping Walsh would elaborate, but he did not. He looked back at her, waiting for an actual question.

"Well, I just wondered what happened there," Shelby pressed.

"Most people don't realize Sofie and I grew up together." Walsh lifted one side of his mouth in a near-grin. "Our families have been friends for thirty years. Our fathers are business partners. So, we did date for a while, but our friendship goes back a long way. She's still the goodwill ambassador for the Walsh Foundation. She's a great girl, and I have only good things to say about her. I think she'd say the same about me."

"Yes, well, there was a lot of speculation that maybe there was someone else."

Again Walsh offered only an unblinking stare, his mouth a straight, neutral line. He shifted, propping his elbow on the arm of the chair and tucking his chin into the palm of his hand, waiting for Shelby to continue.

"*Is* there someone else?" Shelby asked, her eyes braver than the uncertain tone of her voice.

Walsh paused, glancing down before looking back at Shelby. Kerris wondered if anyone else detected the shutters he had just pulled over his eyes.

"Like you said, it's been quite a year. I haven't had a lot of time for much besides work and doing my part with the foundation."

"So there's no one special?" Shelby fished, using her grin as bait.

"There are many special women in the world." Walsh offered a scrap metal smile, giving Shelby nothing new to work with. "Just not for me right now."

"If you *were* ready for your someone special, what would she be like?"

Walsh lowered a thick fan of lashes, concealing his eyes. Concealing his thoughts. For a moment it seemed he wouldn't answer Shelby's question, but then he looked back up, and there was an unexpected intensity in his eyes.

"She'd be compassionate. She'd be someone with a strong sense of what's right, and doing what is right, no matter what. She'd be loyal and fearless."

Shelby leaned forward, obviously thrilled that the usually reticent Walsh Bennett was revealing so much.

"And beautiful?"

"It would be incidental." Walsh pushed his broad shoulders into a dismissive shrug. "The qualities I'd be looking for are... elusive. Rare."

"Have you ever met a woman who embodied all these things?"

"Yes," Walsh said without pause, his face a riddle no one would be able to solve. His quick smile, the answer. "My mother."

Kerris hastily wiped the tears she hadn't meant to shed. She turned the TV off, jumping at the sound of Al Green crooning "Call Me (Come Back Home)," the ring tone Cam had chosen for his phone. She doubted he had one song from this century in his collection. If it wasn't on vinyl, he didn't want it. She glanced around the room, searching for his phone before she realized the sound was coming from the office. She grabbed it in case he was calling looking for it. The ringing stopped abruptly, replaced by the ding signaling he had a new text message.

I told you I had something special for you. Call me when you get this.

A picture came through of a blonde, her face partially obscured by the T-shirt she was raising to expose her naked breasts. Nausea tensed the muscles of Kerris's stomach. She swallowed a lump comprised of hurt and shame and inadequacy and indignation. They had barely been intimate over the last few weeks. She'd thought it was the pregnancy and the memory of Walsh between them, but maybe this was the real reason.

Was this how Cam felt when he walked in on that kiss? Betrayed? Angry? Helpless?

A car door slammed. Kerris peered through the office window. Cam climbed out of his pride and joy, the Land Rover Kristeene had left him. He stopped by the battered old Camry Kerris insisted on keeping, inspecting the tires and frowning before heading down the walk toward the cottage door.

"Ker, I'm home." She heard Cam open the refrigerator and then the stove. "I'm starving. You cook or want me to order something?"

Kerris walked toward the kitchen, looking for the wisdom and the strength to handle this properly. She watched Cam riffling through the menus in the junk drawer.

"You need new tires, by the way. I'll get 'em." Cam studied a menu and patted the pocket of the jeans hanging low on his lean hips. "You hungry? I'm gonna call my order in."

Kerris watched him pat his jeans again and then walk back into the living room, searching for his phone. Kerris held it up.

"Looking for this?" She leaked anger in her tone, saving the hurt for later.

A look of relief washed over his face.

"Yeah, I was. The day was so crazy I just realized I didn't have it." He extended his hand, palm open. When she held on to the phone, Cam frowned. "Ker, my phone."

"Why?" Kerris willed her voice not to wobble. "Afraid I'll see something I shouldn't? Like a message from your friend?"

His dark brows jerked together over confused eyes that might have convinced her before, but not anymore.

"Who?"

Kerris turned the phone around, making sure he got the eyeful that had been intended for him. Cam scanned the screen and then rolled his eyes.

"Baby, that's just some girl from the office. She's a piece of work. Sorry you had to see that, but I barely know her."

He wiggled his fingers for the phone, but Kerris wasn't ready to release the evidence.

"Really, Cam?" Kerris threaded her voice with disdain. "You think I'm buying that?"

"I know how it must look, but I promise you I haven't done anything with that chick." Cam ran his long fingers through the dark hair spilling around his ears. "Not 'cause she hasn't tried. Geesh, she's persistent. I'll make sure she doesn't pull a stunt like that again."

"A stunt?" Kerris scoffed, a disbelieving whoosh of air escaping from her chest. "The only stunt is the one you're trying to pull on me right now."

Cam's eyes flinted and the muscle in his lean jaw flexed.

"You don't believe me?"

"Why should I?"

"Maybe because when I saw you with my *own eyes* kissing my best friend I stayed. I chose to trust you when you said it wouldn't happen again." Cam dropped his hand, clenching it at his side. "Scroll through the history and see all the messages I've exchanged with her."

Kerris glanced down at the phone, rolling her thumb over the screen to pull down other messages.

Nothing. Just the picture she had sent to Cam right before he'd walked in the door.

"You could have deleted them."

"What's her name?"

"What?"

"What's her name?" Cam gestured to the phone. "Is she saved as a contact in my phone, or is it just some random number and a set of fake tits?"

Kerris, a sick feeling roiling her stomach, looked back at the phone. No name. Just a number. Maybe...

"Cam, I—"

"I swear on my baby growing inside you that I didn't cheat with that girl, or anybody else, since the day you married me." Cam snatched the phone and slid it into his back pocket. "Tell me you see the irony here. I had a lot more reason not to trust you than you had, and yet here we are. You accusing me of cheating."

"Cam, what was I supposed to think?"

"I don't know." Cam shrugged broad shoulders under his cotton button-up. "That my vows actually mean something to me."

"That's not fair. They mean something to me, too."

"Apparently, they mean something different to you." A bitter laugh shoved its way past Cam's lips. "The crazy thing is everybody thought you were the good girl marrying the bad boy. Poor Kerris. Cam won't stay faithful, when all along you were the cheat."

His words, so close to the ache she'd felt earlier, missing Walsh, sawed at her heart.

"Don't." Her whisper begged him to stop, even though she knew Cam well enough to know he wouldn't. "You know I'd never cheat on you."

"You mean you'd never fuck Walsh." Cam's beautiful face twisted into something as close to ugly as it could ever come. "Doesn't mean you don't cheat, and it's sad that for a while I was willing to settle for that. Not anymore. Maybe I don't deserve a girl who loves me, but I'd rather be alone than in a marriage with two other people."

"I thought we were past this." Kerris swallowed the regret and shame crawling up her throat. "I'm sorry. I shouldn't have confronted you that way—"

"Oh, I know exactly why you shot first and asked questions later." Cam's expression calcified. "You were looking for a way out."

"No." Kerris gestured to her swollen belly. "I'm pregnant. You think I'd want something like that to happen?"

"Either way, you got it. I'm done. I can't do this anymore, Ker."

"You're giving up?" Desperation choked the breath from Kerris's lungs. Every word out of Cam's mouth stabbed a hole in the dream she was this close to having—a family. "We haven't really tried."

"Haven't tried? What do you think this has been?"

"I mean really tried. Like talk to someone. Maybe go to counseling."

"Counseling?" Cam went still and stiff. "You know I don't do shrinks."

"I was thinking more a marriage counselor." Kerris took a step in Cam's direction, softening her voice for the next words. "And maybe they could recommend someone for you."

"For me?" Wariness shuttered Cam's face and slitted his eyes. "I don't need a counselor."

"Cam, your nightmares have only gotten worse and you're barely sleeping."

Cam pointed one long finger in her direction. "Holy fuck! You got some nerve turning this back on me. I don't need a *counselor*. I'm not the one fighting to stay in a marriage I don't even want."

"That's not true."

"What do you want, Kerris?"

"I...well...I want you and...this baby, of course."

"Of course you do." Cam swaddled the words in sarcasm. "Don't make me out to be the head case when you're in love with two guys."

"I'm not."

"Yeah, you're right. You're not in love with two guys. Just one." Cam strode to the door, launching his next words over his shoulder like a torpedo. "Too bad he's not your husband.

He slammed the door behind him.

So sad, so familiar, a door closing. Gone. For a moment, after the violence of their raised voices, Kerris welcomed the silence, but then it throbbed and thickened around her. Swelled in the cottage, lonely and desolate.

Not an affair. Some set of fake tits Cam had called her. That girl meant absolutely nothing to Cam. Echoes of his accusations stung her ears. He was right. She was the cheat because

Walsh did mean something to her. In another life, he would have been the air she breathed. In this one, he was the magnificent thorn piercing her side, tempting her to go against the grain of what she knew was right. She was culpable, responsible for all of the convolutions in this marriage. For the circuitous hurt she continued to do to Cam, even when her intentions were the best.

Moving like an old woman, she shuffled into her bedroom and lay on the bed. She didn't bother removing the kimono, but just slipped under the covers and went to sleep.

> *"If you were ready for your someone special, what would she be like?"*
>
> *Walsh looked away from Shelby's probing stare and directly into Kerris's eyes. He smiled that slow smile she'd never seen him give to anyone else, reaching out to tangle his long fingers with hers. He pulled Kerris to him, towering over her, sheltering her. She had missed this feeling. In these few moments, she forgot about Shelby. Forgot about the world outside of these arms. There was only now. There was only them, and things were right. She wasn't sure how it had happened, but things were finally right.*
>
> *Walsh whispered her name like an incantation.*
>
> *Kerris. Kerris. Kerris.*

"Kerris!"

"Walsh," she muttered, still clawing her way out of the dream. She sat up in bed, rubbing her eyes and pulling the kimono close around her neck.

"What'd you just call me?" Cam stood in the semidark, the lamp illuminating the mounting rage on his face.

"Cam! Oh, gosh. No. No, it's not…not—" she sputtered, still blinking heavy sleep from her eyes.

"In your sleep!" Cam chopped a stiff hand through the air and leaned down until their noses almost touched. "And you have the nerve to accuse me of cheating? When you lie down beside me every night and dream about *him*?"

His hot, alcohol-soaked breath fanned her face. words were not crisp, but slurred, slopping around in his mouth, crowded out by anger and outrage.

"Cam, you've been drinking." With false calm, she reached up to touch his face, wiping at the dampness on his forehead. "It's been a volatile night for us both. Let's talk about this tomorrow when we're both in our right minds."

Cam pushed her hand away.

"Oh, I'm finally in my right mind. I came back to talk things through. Give it one more chance, at least for the baby's sake, but I had it right the first time. I'm done."

He strode to the door, not looking back. The last she heard of him was the slamming door. Again. A tired déjà vu of earlier tonight. Of so many slammed doors and violent departures over the course of her life.

She sat for a moment just as he'd left her, blinking in the dim light and rubbing at arms chilled from the air conditioning. Chilled from the finality of his parting words. And then it hit her. Cam had been drinking. He was angry. He was driving away. She had to stop him.

She scrambled out of the bed, not even bothering to throw on shoes. She snatched her keys and her purse and dashed toward her Camry, realizing it was raining only when she slid on the wet cobblestones.

She pulled out onto the road, training her eyes on the taillights of the Land Rover ahead of her. She struggled to remain calm. Cam was still within sight. Irrational as it was, she felt that as long as she kept him within sight, she could protect him. She could at least be there if a cop stopped him. She rubbed her stomach and pressed the accelerator as much as she dared, needing to get a little closer.

"Hold on, little one."

The rain came down harder now, faster than her decrepit wipers could keep pace. She squinted through the sheets of rain pummeling her windshield before finally turning her bright lights on. She grabbed her phone, glancing down to select Cam's contact. The phone rang several times before finally rolling into voice mail.

She tossed her phone back into her purse, setting a grate over the fear and panic that burned in her belly and throat.

"Cameron Mitchell, when this is all over, I'm gonna kill you."

Cam veered sharply to the left, avoiding something in the road. Kerris pulled her steering wheel to avoid it, too, but she immediately felt her tires spinning free of the road; she could feel the unresponsive steering wheel sliding through her hands as she spun once and then again and then again and then again. There was no last thought when she cannoned toward the tree with its menacing limbs. All thoughts were drowned out by the scream that erupted from her throat, filling the car before it dissolved into the deathly silence that remained.

Chapter Four

Kerris is in the hospital!"

Meredith rubbed her eyes, struggling to drag herself from the warmth of her down comforter and a deep sleep.

"Cam?" She ran her hands through her tuft of spiky hair, her voice sleep-slurred. "Is that you?"

"Yes. Yes." His words popped out between panicked breaths. "Did you hear me? Kerris is in the hospital. It's all my fault, Mer. Oh, God!"

"Whoa, whoa, whoa." Meredith sat up, reaching beside the bed to snap on the lamp. "What are you saying?"

"She's in the hospital. Rivermont General."

"What happened?" Fear squeezed the muscles of her throat, barely letting the words out.

"She was…she was coming after me." Cam's voice broke over the last word.

"I don't understand." Meredith frowned and threw the covers back. She rushed toward her closet, grabbing the first pair of jeans she reached, pulling them on under her nightshirt and not even bothering with a bra.

"We had a—" Cam stopped, pausing to draw a shallow, anxious breath. "We had a fight, and I had been drinking. I drove out, and she came after me."

Meredith paused in pulling on her Uggs, longing to dive through the phone and squish the life from Cam.

"You sorry piece of shit." Meredith snatched up her bag and keys, bolting from the apartment.

"I know." Cam groaned, his voice holding all the torture she hoped he was feeling. "I know. Just…just come."

"Oh, don't you worry." She slammed her car door, looking over her shoulder to zip out of the parking lot. "I'm on my way."

Twenty minutes later, she almost felt sorry that she had been so hard on Cam when she saw him slumped in the plastic chair, head flopping into his hands, anguish in every line of his body.

"Cam." She tapped him on the shoulder. "Talk to me."

He raised his head, eyes already red-rimmed and swollen from tears.

"She…she…it's bad."

"Where is she?" Meredith hoped she sounded more confident than she felt. She'd never seen Cam like this. Even when Kristeene Bennett died, his eyes hadn't held this kind of despondency.

"She's in surgery." He ran a trembling hand through his tumble of dark hair.

"Surgery?" Meredith gulped, afraid to ask the question. "And the baby?"

"They're doing an emergency C-section now." Defeat weighted his shoulders. "Our chances aren't very good."

"Not very good? For Kerris? For the baby?"

"For either of them." He dropped his head back into his hands. "Oh, God, Meredith. What if they don't make it?"

Meredith's heart pounded in her chest so hard it hurt, like she couldn't draw breath fast or deep enough. This was when Kerris's mother should have been here to pray and believe with a mother's defiant faith. But Kerris didn't have that, and Meredith felt her absence.

"Cam, have you called Mama Jess?"

"No." Cam sniffed, wiping his nose with the back of his hand. "I didn't…I don't have her number."

Meredith pulled her phone from her purse and searched her contacts. "Dammit."

"What?" Cam raised his head again to peer at her through the hair drooping in his eyes.

"I don't have her number either." She sucked her teeth in frustration. "How is that even possible?"

"You think it'll be in Kerris's phone?"

"I'm sure it would be." She clicked through her contacts once more, even though she knew it was pointless.

"I have her purse." Cam reached behind the chair to pass the bag Meredith recognized immediately as Kerris's. "The cops gave it to me."

She grabbed it, rifling through the contents until she found Kerris's phone. She scrolled down to find Mama Jess's number, pausing over another contact along the way. Trisha McAvery. She recognized the name. Kerris had told her Walsh's assistant, Trisha McAvery, admired her bracelet and was taking it to a friend in New York who might be interested in buying.

She called Mama Jess, providing the few details she could before urging the older woman to come. Meredith glanced up at

Cam, head still in his hand, foot tapping a restless rhythm on the waiting room floor. Meredith stalked around the corner and down to the ladies' restroom, slipping into the handicapped stall. She started dialing, letting the door slam shut behind her. After three rings, Meredith was about to hang up or hope for a voice mail.

"Hello?" a sleep-heavy voice asked from the other end. "Kerris?"

Trisha must have Kerris programmed in her phone, too.

"No, this is actually Kerris's best friend, Meredith."

"Do you have any idea what time it is, Meredith? It's freaking two o'clock in the morning."

"Sorry about that." Meredith bit her lip, hoping this wasn't crazy. "I wouldn't call if it wasn't an emergency. And Walsh's number isn't in Kerris's phone."

There was a loaded silence before she heard Trisha speak again, her tone more alert.

"Has something happened to Kerris, Meredith?"

"Yes."

"Oh, God. Is she okay?"

"No."

"Is she alive?"

"She is, but it's bad." Meredith swiped at an errant tear. "I thought…well, she and Walsh…they're—"

"Yes, I understand and you're right." It sounded like Trisha was now in motion. "Walsh would want to know. Tell me everything."

* * *

Three bangs on his door. Insistent. Successive.

Walsh creaked his eyes open, sat up, and glanced around his bedroom, struggling to orient himself. He'd been in negotiations with Sheikh Kassim all day about a possible merger, and well into the night. Walsh glanced at the watch on his wrist. He'd been asleep for only an hour or so.

The banging came again. Whoever stood on the other side of that door should prepare for his sleep-deprived wrath. Walsh dragged on pajama bottoms, grumbling and stumbling his way to the door.

"Who the hell is it?"

"It's Trisha."

Walsh swung the door open and narrowed his eyes on his assistant, standing in the hallway outside his apartment.

"Trisha, this better be good."

"I need to tell you something."

"In the middle of the night?" He stepped back to allow her inside.

She stepped into the modern luxury of his apartment. She'd been there only a few times, usually to drop something off from the office. She eyed the large black-and-white photo of his mother hanging over his fireplace. She pressed her eyes shut for a moment before opening them to meet his stare.

"Out with it, Trish."

"When I first started working for you, you gave me a short list of people. You said to find you if they ever needed you, no matter what."

Walsh's eyes slitted and his body tightened. If anything had happened to anyone on that list, he'd lose it.

"What's this about?"

"It's Kerris."

The words landed in his chest like a meteor, cratering his composure and stealing his air. He couldn't form the question. Her answer could decimate him. He relished the last few seconds of not knowing for sure. He looked at Trish with a steady, waiting intensity.

"There's been an accident."

"No."

"Yes, Walsh she—"

"Do *not* say she's dead." He shook his head and swallowed convulsively. "Don't tell me that."

"No, Walsh," she rushed to correct. "But she's badly injured."

"How do you know?"

"Her friend Meredith called me."

He leaned against the wall, propping his head against it and holding her eyes.

"What happened?"

"A car accident."

"But she's alive? And the baby?"

"It doesn't look good...for either of them."

"No, I don't believe that. She's strong."

"Walsh, her car hydroplaned and slammed into a tree."

"Oh, God." He slid to the floor, sitting with his back to the wall and his elbows on his knees. His head fell between his arms, his hand reaching behind his neck to grip it as if holding on for dear life.

"She's in surgery now. They're performing an emergency C-section trying to save the baby."

Walsh's head snapped up, eyes pinning Trisha to the spot.

"What about Kerris?"

Trisha squatted, resting on her haunches, clasping her hands dangling between her knees. "She has internal injuries. Her window shattered, and a limb from the tree pierced her side."

Walsh moaned, a shudder shredding through his chest. He sprang to his feet and strode back to his bedroom.

"You said Meredith called you, right?"

"Um, yeah."

"Send me her contact. I need to get to Rivermont like an hour ago."

"Your father has the Bennett jet, but I'll check on the next available flight." She stopped at the entrance to his bedroom, watching him stuff clothes haphazardly into his Louis Vuitton carryall.

"I'll call Sheikh Kassim." Walsh trimmed his voice of everything but determination. "He has a private jet. I want it ready to go within the hour."

"Walsh, do you have any idea what time it is? I know you're anxious to get there, but you can't just wake a sheikh up at this hour and expect him to jump through hoops for you."

He reached for his cell phone on his bedside table without sparing Trisha a glance.

"Watch me."

Walsh clenched his jaw, faltering for a moment. Standing still as he fought against the mess of emotions flooding him. Kerris had bisected his life into two chunks. Before her and after her. Even though he wasn't allowed into her life, she was everything. If he thought too long about a world where she no longer existed, he'd dissolve.

"I just…" Whatever was in his eyes, he didn't try to hide it from Trisha when he finally looked at her. "I just need to get there."

She walked further into the room and grabbed the phone from him.

"You finish packing. I'll call him myself."

Chapter Five

W hat are you looking for?" Mama Jess crinkled her brow, studying Meredith's face.

"Hmmm?" Meredith glanced at the entrance to the waiting room again and again. She swung her eyes back around to Mama Jess. "What'd you ask me?"

"I said what—"

Meredith's phone rang and she snatched it from her back pocket.

"'Scuse me, Mama Jess." She glanced down at the screen, leaping to her feet and speeding around the corner.

"Hello," Meredith said, her voice tentative, waiting for the unidentified caller to speak.

"Meredith," Walsh said from the other end, sounding about as weary and worried as she did. "How is she?"

"Where are you?" She answered his question with one of her

own, glancing over her shoulder and being careful not to say his name.

"I just landed at Raleigh-Durham. I'm on my way there now."

"No, you can't." Meredith slipped into the stall she'd used before to call Trish. "I wanted you to know, but I didn't intend for you to come here."

"And did you honestly think there was anyone who could keep me from coming?" Walsh asked, his voice weary and implacable. "I'm not concerned about what you or Cam or anyone else thinks right now. I'm coming. Try to stop me."

She closed her eyes, hearing the steel in his voice. Oh, God, what had she done? She didn't know exactly what had gone wrong between the two men, but she knew Kerris was at the center of it. Cam was a sloppy mess in the waiting room, drowning in guilt and frustration. He wasn't stable. If Walsh showed up now, there was no telling what would happen. It was a volatile powder keg, and she had just lit a fuse.

"Walsh, let's compromise."

"I'm making no promises. And I *will* see her."

"No one can see her right now. She's still in surgery."

"And the baby?"

Meredith clutched the handicap stall grab bar for support before sinking to sit on the closed toilet seat. The silence ripened while she looked for words.

"Meredith?" Walsh's voice was more quiet, less certain.

"The baby didn't make it."

"Oh, God. Does she know yet?"

"No, she hasn't been conscious since they brought her in. They did the C-section, but the baby was already...was already gone. Then they took Kerris into surgery for the internal injuries she's sustained."

"Fuck!" She heard Walsh bang something with force. And then bang it again. "I'm coming to that hospital. I don't care how it looks. Not you, not Cam, nobody will stop me."

"It won't do any good for you to be here right now." Meredith smothered the words in persuasion. "She's in surgery, and if you come, you and Cam will just glare and circle each other like wild dogs."

"How is he?" Concern softened Walsh's voice.

"He's suffering."

"I can only imagine. No, I can't imagine. He has to be grieving for the baby, and still waiting for Kerris to come out of surgery."

"And the guilt," Meredith added before she could stop herself, biting her lip. She practically heard the cogs in that sharp mind on the other end turning.

"What does he have to feel guilty about?" Something quiet and deadly slid into Walsh's voice.

"Um…"

"Don't even think about lying to me. What are you not telling me?"

"Walsh—"

"I'll find out, so just tell me now."

"Well, they had a fight."

"Uh-huh."

"And apparently Cam…"

"Cam what?"

"Cam had been drinking and stormed off. Kerris was scared he'd hurt himself, so she went after him, and it was raining. There was something in the road. She veered and hydroplaned."

The details tumbled out in a rush, the waiting stillness on the other end making Meredith wish she could take back every word before they reached his ears.

"And you expect me to back off for him?" His words were so soft and ominous, a shiver of fear ran along her arms. "If she dies, Meredith, I'll twist that pretty face of his beyond recognition."

"Walsh, listen."

"No compromise. I'm on my way."

"Okay, okay." Meredith's shoulders dropped another inch. "But call me when you get here. Wait in the parking lot. I'll come out to let you know what's up, and we can go from there."

She held her breath, waiting for his response.

"Okay, Walsh? Can you at least do that for me?"

She heard a car door slam.

"I'm on my way."

She'd have to take that as a yes.

* * *

Walsh sat in the parking lot, considering the hospital entrance, so quiet at this time of morning, the sun just starting to overtake the night sky. The last time he'd been here, it had been to take his mother home to die. And before that, there had been Iyani. Kerris had been by his side through that ordeal.

He smiled, remembering how they had distracted each other that day with silly jokes and teasing as they'd waited during Iyani's surgery. They'd laughed over his mother's soul food. His mind had greedily hoarded every moment he'd ever spent with her, and it was like bread and water to him now—sustaining. What if he never saw her alive again? He slammed his fist into the steering wheel, wishing it were Cam's head.

Thoughtless. Selfish. Foolish. Irresponsible.

He had known Cam could be all those things, and he'd bowed out anyway, let him walk off with a treasure he had known was meant to be his. He really didn't know if he was angriest at Cam or at himself. He pulled out his phone.

"Meredith, I'm here." He kept his voice low and free of the wretched emotion boring a hole in his gut.

"I'm coming out," she whispered back. "Where are you?"

"There's a G on the pole in front of me. Does that help?"

"Yeah, I'll see you in a sec."

A few minutes later, Walsh unlocked the car door, and Meredith slid into the passenger seat.

"Hi, Walsh." She looked at him like he was a booby trap, poised to go off with one misstep. She wasn't wrong.

"How is she?"

"Still in surgery."

"What are we dealing with?"

"Well, of course her car was ancient. No side air bags, so she really bore the brunt of it when she slammed into that tree. A huge limb came through the window. Four ribs on her left side are broken. Her left lung was punctured and has collapsed. Her left arm and leg are broken."

Meredith fixed a flat gaze on the windshield ahead of her.

"She hit her head against the side of the window, but we don't know the impact of that yet. It seems that there wasn't much damage to her face. Just some surface scratches and cuts from the shattered glass and branches."

Meredith had cataloged Kerris's injuries dispassionately, almost matter-of-factly. She didn't fool him, though. Walsh saw the tremble in her fingers and noted the sharp marks where she had bitten her lip too hard. The same terror that gripped him gripped her.

"How're you holding up?" Walsh reached over to squeeze her hand.

"I…I'm," she started and stopped with a flurry of blinks to stem her tears. "I'm fine."

"You're a wreck."

Her face crumpled, tears rolling down her cheeks unchecked. "I'm a wreck. I'm so scared, Walsh."

"Me, too."

The words were a breath, all the sound he could spare with fear holding him in a headlock. He gathered her close, offering the comfort he needed for himself. He allowed her to cry a few minutes, releasing some of the strain and trepidation that had been locked inside her for the last few hours. He finally pulled back, peering into her tear-splotched face.

"Better?"

"Not really." She choked on a half-laugh, half-cry.

"I didn't think so." Walsh drummed his fingers on the steering wheel. "Tell me how this needs to go."

"If Cam sees you, it won't be good."

"Yeah, well if I see him it won't be good." A growly rumble, Walsh's voice held the threat of a violent storm. "She was chasing him after a fight? And he was drunk? He's supposed to take care of her."

"Accidents happen." Meredith shifted in the passenger seat, her fingers plucking at the seat belt. He could see all over her face that she didn't buy that line of crap. "He couldn't have known she would follow him out like that."

"This is Kerris we're talking about." He squeezed the steering wheel. "Did he honestly think she would let him drive drunk?"

"I don't think he was thinking."

"That isn't good enough. Dammit, if she dies…"

The silence following his outburst was almost too painful to

sit through. He hoped the fire in his eyes cloaked the bleak desolation enveloping him.

"You love her," Meredith whispered.

He looked straight ahead through the windshield, not acknowledging her.

"You knew the night before their wedding."

"Don't, Walsh."

"Don't what? Remind you that if you had stopped it she might
not be fighting for her life right now?"

"And you?" Meredith fired back. "You could've stopped it at
any time. You knew she lo—"

Walsh swiveled a glance at Meredith when she cut herself off.

"Actually I didn't know how she felt until later, but I couldn't
deny there was something special between us. She did enough
denying for the both of us, though, and I let her get away with it.
I'll never forgive myself for that."

Walsh ignored the burn of tears in his nostrils, gulping back
a useless moan. He laid his forehead against the steering wheel,
rolling his head back and forth.

"Walsh, you can't go in there."

He raised his head, loading the glare he leveled at Meredith with
every bit of frustration and anger he felt before pulling the trigger.

"The hell I can't."

"Right now, no one can see her." Meredith laid a staying hand
on his arm. "And until anyone can see her, I just think you being
in the waiting room will only agitate Cam."

Cam deserved every drop of guilt he was probably choking on
right now. Walsh wasn't worried about him.

"Look, my family practically built this hospital," Walsh said.
"I'll find somewhere to hang out. Just call me as soon as she's out
of surgery."

Walsh pulled out his cell phone, watching Meredith slip back through the hospital entrance. Good, he still had Dr. Ravenscroft's number. Not even considering the lateness—or earliness—of the hour, he dialed it.

"Dr. Ravenscroft here." His mother's old physician sounded as alert as he always did.

"Dr. Ravenscroft, it's Walsh Bennett. Sorry to call so early, but I need a huge favor."

* * *

Half an hour later, Walsh walked into what would soon be the Kristeene Walsh Bennett Cancer Wing, carefully picking his way around a few piles of unfinished lumber. It was still under construction, but Dr. Ravenscroft had assured Walsh that at least one office, his own, was close enough to completion for him to crash there for a while. He followed the doctor's instructions, taking the needed turns that brought him to an office that was, even though not quite finished, obviously going to be luxuriously appointed. Well, a hospital's version of luxuriously appointed. Dr. Ravenscroft would have some real office envy if he ever got a load of Martin Bennett's Persian rug.

It occurred to him that he had fled New York in the midst of crucial negotiations with Sheikh Kassim.

"I'll have to call Dad," he said to the empty room.

Someone else could step in for a few…days? Weeks? He wasn't sure how long Kerris would be unconscious, but he wasn't leaving until she wasn't. He'd call Trisha, too. He quirked his lips in a wry smile, remembering Trisha pounding on his door in the middle of the night. He had barely ever spoken about Kerris at all, much less let on how completely his best friend's wife owned him. How had Trisha known?

He flopped down on the leather couch, one of the few pieces of furniture already in the room, and leaned back, feeling the flight and the sleepless night catching up to his body. Sleep wasn't even a possibility, but at least he could close his eyes and rest. Only there was no rest. He had never felt so unsettled. Paradoxically, he felt compelled to move at the same time he longed for an anchor to hold him still and secure. He stood to his feet and headed toward the chapel. It was worth a try.

He sank into the front pew in the empty chapel and shook his head, silently deriding himself. Who was he fooling? He couldn't remember the last time he'd been in a church. He did believe in God, but that was about it. He didn't know that it would do him any good right now. He struggled to recall a prayer, a catechism, a hymn—any tradition that was supposed to make him feel a connection of some kind.

He had nothing.

His mind, his heart, his soul, his spirit were all consumed with fear and a wretched helplessness he couldn't stand. This wasn't something he could conquer or subdue or manipulate or charm. Kerris's life was out of his hands, hanging in the balance, and there was nothing he could do about it. He leaned forward, turning his head so his temple rested against the pew.

It was too much.

He drew several shallow breaths, rehearsing all the hurts he'd endured, situations that had been out of his control and had all ended tragically, leaving him stumbling and grappling. His parents' divorce. Iyani's lost battle. His mother's death, which had left him empty of everything that had held him together.

And Kerris. Losing her hadn't been a physical death, but it was a gradual, ongoing demise of hope. Hope that someone would see him and know him—dark and light, good and bad, and still love him deeply. Nothing would ever convince him that Kerris was not that one. He'd held the cards in his hand and had misplayed them.

All these hurts had been like small tears, tiny rips in the fabric of his soul that had stretched into a gaping hole. Left unattended and unrepaired, they now threatened to swallow him entirely. If Kerris died, he couldn't help but think it would leave him slashed open, permanently, irreparably torn. Like his father when his mother died. Assured and confident and certain on the outside, but beneath—adrift, lost, his certainty the hardened crust around a center turned to mush from irretrievable loss.

And then the words Walsh had heard his father say over and over at his mother's deathbed rested on his lips. Silent at first and then approaching a whisper and then swelling to a moan that filled the cavernous chapel, the syllables melting from the heat of his pain until only he recognized the words. Aloud, it was the incoherent lament he'd heard from his father.

Lost, so lost. Please don't go.

And then he was begging, begging a God he barely knew.

Don't take her. Please, spare her.

It was not a song or a prayer or a tradition, but his original, personal pain that left him, even sitting erect, prostrate. Desperate.

He stood, mopping his wet cheeks without self-consciousness. He turned to leave, startled to see a dark-skinned woman leaning against the wall by the chapel entrance, her arms laid neatly behind her, hands pressed to the wall. He recognized her immediately from Cam's Facebook pictures and posts. It had been

Kerris's birthday, and her happy face had been pressed against this woman's. This was Mama Jess, the foster mother Kerris had told him so much about. Irrationally, Walsh wanted to hurl himself at her, throw his arms around her neck, and weep; he wanted to ask her to make it better. He cleared his throat, burning and raw from his sobs.

"Hi. Um...sorry about that."

She didn't respond, only continued watching, her eyes conducting a thorough, silent inquisition.

"I saw your interview," she said, making Walsh blink his still-wet eyes a few times.

"Excuse me?"

"You were on TV last night. You're Walsh Bennett, right?"

"Yes, ma'am." He moved toward her, feeling like a toddler taking its first few wobbling steps, legs weak and new. "I'm...um a friend of Cam's."

"He could use one right about now. Their baby didn't make it."

"I heard." He gulped back the liquid pain flooding his throat, refusing to show any more weakness than he already had.

"It was a girl."

It was Walsh's turn to remain silent, looking back at her, waiting and wanting more from this woman whom Kerris had rediscovered just in time.

"She's out of surgery." Mama Jess turned to walk away without another word. He had taken the first step after her, ready to demand more when his phone vibrated in his pocket.

"Meredith, what's up?"

"She's out."

Walsh took a deep breath, experiencing a measure of peace he hadn't realized he'd gained in the last ten minutes. He had lived his life getting his way, and forcing it when necessary. For once, he found the strength to hang back and follow the dictates of someone else.

"What do you want me to do?"

"What...um." Meredith faltered. He figured she was unprepared for his docility. "I, well, I was going to suggest you wait until Cam goes home, and then I would get you in for a few minutes. Everything's so complicated. I just don't think him seeing you right now would help anything."

"I can do that. When do you think he'll leave?"

"Everyone's trying to convince him to go home to get a little rest. He's pretty messed up about the baby. Jo's the only one he's really tolerating. I think she's gonna drive him home after he sees Kerris."

"When will that be?"

"She hasn't been out long. It'll be another hour or so before he can see her. She's still not breathing on her own."

Walsh clenched his teeth until his jaw hurt. Kerris couldn't manage something as essential as breathing on her own. He wanted to crawl into her chest and fill it with his own breath. He'd give her his last breath if he could.

"Have you slept? Eaten?" Meredith's concern reached him even over the phone. "Where are you?"

"At the chapel. I have a few things I need to do." Walsh ran a tired hand over the strained muscles in the back of his neck. "I left several loose ends in New York. I'm not going back until she's out of the woods. So, not sure how long you're gonna try to keep my presence here a secret from Cam, but it could get difficult."

"I figured as much." She gave the sigh of an old, weary woman. Mediating between him and Cam wouldn't be easy. "But you haven't seen him. When he found out the baby didn't make it, he just collapsed. He's just...I've never seen him like this."

Walsh's heart didn't even contract. It was Cam's recklessness that had put Kerris here, unable to even breathe on her own. If Walsh opened the door to sympathy, all the other emotions would come storming in, and he couldn't promise that he'd be able to control the violent impulses those would expose. The rage, frustration, and bitterness. A lifetime of it never vented was barely held in check against the man who had been like a brother, but who right now felt like his mortal enemy.

Chapter Six

Walsh cast a furtive glance around the waiting room, searching for Meredith. He spotted her by the elevators. She was expecting him to climb off one of them at any moment, but he had taken the stairs.

"Meredith."

She jumped a little and turned toward him, her face tired and tight.

"Come this way." She ran a hand over her choppy, bright hair. "We don't have long. Everyone's gone home, but they'll be back. I told them I'd stay and let them know if there was any change."

"How long?" He followed closely behind her hurried pace.

"Maybe fifteen minutes." She glanced over her shoulder, her eyes making a silent apology. "No one can see her longer than that anyway. Only family's supposed to be allowed in, and only one at a time, but she doesn't really have family per se, other than Cam."

Walsh couldn't help but resent that, technically, Cam had a right to watch over her and he didn't. Walsh had forfeited that when he stepped aside. Meredith stopped at Kerris's hospital room, leaning back against the closed door, looking up at him from more than a foot below.

"Walsh, she's not breathing on her own."

"I know."

"She has several broken bones."

"Yeah, you told me."

"And there's lots of bruising and scratches and cuts."

Walsh measured his words in careful doses, despite the rabid dog inside him straining against the leash, desperate to get on the other side of that door.

"Meredith, I appreciate you calling me. But if you don't get out of my way, I will physically pick you up and move you."

"I'm just trying to prepare you." Tears slid down her feline cheekbones. "It's not pretty."

"Pretty?" His voice was low and hoarse from tears and fatigue. Irritation and impatience jerked his brows into a scowl. "Is that why you think I love her? Because she's pretty?"

"It's not that. She's just—"

"It's Kerris." Enough said. "How will this work? Will you stand guard or something?"

She nodded and stepped aside. Walsh walked in, careful not to look in the direction of the bed until the door was firmly closed behind him. His knees shook and he put a steadying hand out to the wall at his first sight of her. The first time he had seen her, he had marveled at how petite she was. He couldn't help but wish now that she were bigger, stronger, less fragile. In the big hospital bed, she seemed like a broken flower, lost among a weeded network of tubes, wires, and beeping machinery.

He crossed to the chair beside her bed, sitting back, afraid to touch her. He lowered his forehead to the bed rail, needing its coolness against his fevered skin. Slowly he extended his hand to touch her little fingers, his hand literally twice the size of hers. The arm and leg on the other side were already plastered. Abrasions and cuts marred her beautiful honeyed skin with bruises, bluish and black. Her mouth was held slightly open by the tube snaking inside. Her hair haloed around her on the white pillow, the fire winding through the dark silk subdued in the dim light of the room.

"Hey, baby."

The gruff whisper of his own voice grated on his nerves. He swallowed back the tears he had promised himself he wouldn't indulge.

"I...I know we haven't seen each other in a long time." He squeezed her hand. "I don't want to make things complicated, but nothing could have kept me away. I don't know if you can hear me, but if you can, I hope it's a good thing that I'm here. I can't stay long, but..."

If she couldn't hear him, didn't know he was here, what was the point? Except his own selfish need to be near her, even though he had no right and no one wanted him here; no one thought he should be here.

"I love you, Kerris."

It was unnecessary. There was no way she didn't know that, but he realized he'd told her only once, and then it had almost been an accusation. They'd argued in her kitchen and he'd been furious with her for assuming he was marrying Sofie, for ruining their chance together. He squeezed her hand again, shocked to feel the pressure almost imperceptibly returned.

She'd squeezed his hand!

Meredith thrust her head into the room, her words an uneasy hiss.

"Walsh, it's time to go. Cam's coming."

"Meredith, she just squeezed my hand! That's good, right?"

"Sure, Walsh. It's good. Did you hear me? Cam's coming."

"Okay, hold on."

He turned back to Kerris. He stood and stepped as close as the labyrinth of wires would allow, leaning in until his lips brushed her ear. He spoke low enough for only her to hear.

"Kerris, I know you hear me. Come back to me. You can spend the rest of your life with him. I won't ever pressure you again. Just come back. I can't breathe without you here. I need you. I love you. God, so much."

The rebellious tears finally twisted down his face. He couldn't let the words go. They clung to his tongue, and they kept tumbling out of him over and over like a needle stuck on a record.

"I love you. I love you. I love you."

He wept into her neck, burrowing into her, fortified by the strong, steady pulse beating beneath her skin.

"Walsh!" Meredith's voice snapped a warning, like twigs underfoot. "You have to leave *now*."

He straightened and turned, an apology dying on his lips. He looked over Meredith's shoulder into the bleak hatred on Cam's face.

"What the hell are you doing here?" Cam's eyes cut to the bed, where Kerris lay still.

"What is *she* doing here?" Walsh refused to back down. "Why was she out chasing you in the middle of the night?"

"Wow." Cam struck just the right note of false casualness, leaning back against the wall and crossing his arms over his chest. "You're really well informed for someone who's supposed to be in New York minding his own damn business."

"You know I care about Kerris." Walsh balled his fists in his pockets, holding on to his temper.

"Is that code for I'm in love with your *wife*?" Cam didn't bother turning his head when Meredith gasped.

"She's my friend. How could you not even tell me?"

"Tell you? Tell you! You were supposed to stay out of our lives forever. Did you forget that part? That's still what I want."

"Do you think I give a damn what you want? She was out chasing your sorry drunk ass when this happened. All bets are off."

"You *will* leave." Cam took a menacing step farther into the room.

"And you *will* have to make me." Before Walsh knew it, he had taken a step in Cam's direction.

"Think I can't?"

"You'd have to kill me, Cam, and I don't think even you'd go there."

"You sure about that?" Cam's eyes backed up the dark threat in his voice.

"Okay, stop it," Meredith cut in. "Both of you."

Cam shifted his glare to Meredith.

"And you. You told him, didn't you? No one else knew she came after me. You were the only one I told."

"I thought he should know she was in the hospital."

"Why doesn't anyone remember that she's *my* wife? Mine!"

"You sound like a spoiled child." Walsh's patience was see-through thin by now. "Mine, mine, mine. She's fighting for her life. Can't we put this aside until she's out of the woods?"

"No, we can't put this aside. You wanna fuck my wife."

"Watch your mouth, boy!" Mama Jess snapped from the door, drawing everyone's attention.

Cam turned sheepish eyes to Mama Jess, before glaring back in Walsh's direction.

"Mama Jess, I'm sorry, but you don't understand. This is—"

"I know who it is. You ain't gotta tell me. Both of you need to be quiet."

"With all due respect—" Cam began.

"What you know about respect?" Mama Jess's hands rested on her round hips. "I heard you. She was chasing you? That's why she's here right now?"

"Look, what happens between a man and his wife is private. We had an argument."

"That landed Lil' Bit here." Mama Jess's words were fiery pokers, and though not directed at him, Walsh felt the stinging heat.

"I'm her husband, and if I say you all have to leave, then you all have to leave."

"I've already told you I'm not going anywhere." Walsh pulled every muscle of his face into the mulish lines that had gotten him what he wanted most of his life.

"Both of y'all just be quiet," Mama Jess said. "I mean literally be quiet. Do you hear that?"

The only sound was the steady press of the machine giving breath to Kerris.

"Do you *hear* that?" Mama Jess repeated. "That's a machine breathing for her, and you're having a pissin' contest. I wonder if either of you cares for her at all if you can't get past this long enough to put her first."

A stern-looking nurse chose that moment to come in, raising her eyebrows for a second before pulling them back into a frown.

"I'm sorry. There can be only one person here at a time. And it's only a few minutes at a time."

"I'll go." Walsh headed toward the door, but paused beside Meredith. "Keep me posted?"

Walking through the door, he couldn't resist bending down to kiss Mama Jess on the cheek, despite the frown she still wore. He could have sworn there was a softening in her granite-hard expression.

"Thank you for loving her. And for coming back into her life," he said. "She always loved you like a mother."

"How do you know that?" Mama Jess whispered back, her eyes filling with tears.

"She told me."

* * *

"Hello." Walsh's father responded on the second ring.

"Dad, it's me." Walsh firmed up his tone and corrected his posture.

"Walsh? This is a surprise."

"I, um, I'm in Rivermont." Walsh braced himself for the explosion.

"What about Sheikh Kassim?" His father was much more calm than Walsh had anticipated. "I thought you were in discussions with him all this week there in New York."

"I was. I have been, but something came up and I had to come here."

"Walsh, I don't have to tell you how crucial these negotiations are."

"No, Dad, you don't. There are some things I could get done from here, but some of it has to be face-to-face. I know that."

"What's so important? Something with your mother's estate?"

"No." Walsh clipped the word. He couldn't think about his mother dying with Kerris still fighting that battle only yards away. "Look, I don't know if you've met Cam's wife."

"Kerris."

Her name so readily on his father's lips robbed Walsh of speech for a moment. Not only had his father apparently met Kerris, but remembered her name. There were employees who had retired from Bennett after twenty years of service whose names eluded his father.

"Uh, yeah, Kerris. You've met her?"

"I met her when you were kidnapped." Martin skimmed over the event as if he'd met Kerris at a Christmas party. "She recognized your hands. Or, rather, what were not your hands."

"Huh?"

"Those shitheads from Haiti? They sent us a finger with some of your belongings, implying that it was yours."

"It was Paul's." Walsh's heart sagged beneath the familiar guilt over the missionary his captors had murdered right in front of him. Needlessly.

"Yeah, well, your mother and Jo and even Cameron were all set to start moaning about it." A touch of humor entered Martin's voice. "That little lady, not bigger than a minute, frowned and said, 'That's not his finger.'"

Walsh swallowed, closing his eyes. What woman recognized a man's fingers if she didn't love him just a little bit?

"And then she looked at my hand and said, 'Those are his fingers.'"

Martin gave into a full-bodied chuckle, sounding somewhat delighted.

"Can you believe that? Intense little thing, isn't she?"

"She's been in a car accident." Walsh tried to ignore the stingers of pain in his chest, expelling the next words. "She was pregnant and has already lost the baby. It's bad. I'm not leaving until she's out of the woods."

"You there to support Cameron?" Walsh knew his father was more than merely curious.

"I'm here for her." Walsh slathered the remark with defiance. He was not in the mood to defend his feelings for Kerris.

"That's good. Don't worry about Kassim. I'll put Miller on it."

Walsh wired his jaw shut, squelching the protest that sprang to his lips. Andru Miller, a few years older than Walsh, was ambitious and hungry. He looked for any chance to prove to Martin that he was just as capable and more deserving than Walsh. The thought of Miller cozying up to the sheikh, taking credit at the last minute for the relationship Walsh had spent the last six months cultivating…

"Sounds good," Walsh forced himself to say. "I'll call Trisha so she can get Miller up to speed."

"Hey, son," Martin said. "She's an exceptional girl. Kerris, I mean."

Walsh couldn't speak. Had he ever heard his father apply the word "exceptional" to a person? Steaks were exceptional. Opportunities were exceptional. The coffee he had flown in from Colombia was exceptional. But a woman his father barely knew?

"I know I've always wanted you to marry Sofie," Martin said into the silence Walsh couldn't find a way to break. "But if you married a girl like Kerris, I'd be pleased."

Walsh swallowed the emotion burning and pressing against the inside of his throat.

"Bye, Dad."

"Bye, son."

Chapter Seven

She's breathing on her own," Meredith said into her phone, lowering her voice. She sat down in one of the waiting room's now-too-familiar plastic chairs.

It had been a week since the accident, and the doctors had been justifiably concerned that Kerris still wasn't consistently breathing on her own. The punctured and collapsed lung had definitely complicated things, but this morning she had drawn clear breaths on her own ever since they took her off the ventilator. The doctors seemed to be leveling with them when they said Kerris should be waking up any day now. They couldn't be sure how severe the head injury was until she was awake and they could assess her speech, lucidity, memory, and functionality.

Meredith waited for Walsh's response on the other line. He had stayed away. She knew what it had cost him, but since Mama Jess's rebuke in the room last week, Walsh had not darkened the hospital door again. In exchange, he demanded daily updates.

"That's incredible." Meredith could hear Walsh's voice, nearly devoid of breath and loaded with relief. "That's my girl. She'll wake up soon."

"That's what we're hoping for." Meredith noticed Cam getting off the elevator and walking toward her. "Look, I gotta go."

"Cam?" It sounded like Walsh had tightened a belt around the name.

"Um, yeah. I'll let you know if there're any changes."

"You do that," Walsh said. "And when that happens, I won't stay away. I'll have to see her for myself, awake and responsive, at least once before I go back to New York."

"Gotta go."

Meredith didn't acknowledge his assertion before hanging up. The next time she was lonely on a Saturday night and feeling sorry for herself, she'd remember that having two men in love with you might be worse than having no one at all.

"Hey, Cam. How goes it?"

"Tough." He pressed his lips together and ran a hand over his haggard features. "It's been hard balancing work and being here. They're understanding about it, but I had accounts I was handling. I went ahead and resigned. Just seemed easier for everyone."

"You resigned?"

"Yeah, we have private insurance, and it's pretty good." Cam coupled his assurance with a frown. "So if you're worried about the hospital bill…"

"No, that wasn't it. I just…it's your job. I wasn't expecting you to quit."

Meredith couldn't help but feel she wasn't getting the full story, but the stiff mask of Cam's face warned her not to press.

"Like I said, it's been tough," Cam said. "Thanks for the text, by the way. Breathing on her own, huh? She'll be home before you know it."

Meredith touched his arm to stop him before he entered Kerris's room.

"Cam, are you okay about…about the baby?"

For a moment, Cam's face, the torture in his eyes, broke Meredith's heart. Kerris hadn't revealed many secrets, but Meredith suspected demons chased them both, and Kerris and Cam had been banking on the baby to bring them some measure of peace.

"I can't do this right now." Cam's eyes, already bloodshot, watered. "It's too much to keep together, and if I talk about the baby…I'm fine."

"I'm so sorry." She dared to probe just a little bit more, placing her hand on his arm to stop him. "I know you and Walsh have had a hard time, but—"

The change on Cam's face stopped Meredith. All signs of vulnerability disappeared, like a dark hand had smothered the pain.

"You don't know shit." Cam sifted grit into his voice, hostility in the eyes narrowed on her face. "Do you know how it feels to know your best friend loves your wife? Has a connection with her you can't even touch?"

She stared at him, taken aback by his sudden vehemence.

"And you just couldn't resist running and telling him everything." Cam had peeled away the mask, all signs of sorrow gone, anger on full display. "You brought the devil right to my doorstep."

"Cam, they're friends."

"Friends." Cam shook her hand off, derision shading his voice. "Is that what you call it?"

"I know Kerris has never been unfaithful to you, so don't even imply that."

"How would you feel if you walked in on your husband and best friend crawling down each other's throats? Answer that, then come talk to me about being faithful."

Meredith couldn't hide her stunned expression. The bitter hurt darkening Cam's eyes made a mockery of the small smile crooking his lips.

"Oh, she never told you that's why Walsh and I are done? Wonder what other secrets she's got? Not so perfect after all, is she? When your wife doesn't love you, faithful is over-rated."

* * *

"Awake?" Walsh pressed, making sure he'd heard Meredith correctly. "She's awake, you said?"

"Um, yeah." Something in Meredith's tone was more reserved and less approving than he had ever heard. "I just thought you'd want to know."

"You thought I'd want to know? That's an understatement. I've been camped out here for a week waiting for this."

"Yeah, about that. Can I ask you something?"

Walsh paused in packing up his laptop and files.

"Sure, what's up?"

"Cam said something today that kind of threw me for a loop. He asked me how I'd feel if I walked in on my husband and best friend down each other's throats."

"Do you have something to ask me, Meredith?"

"I think I just did."

"Ask me a direct question and I'll give you a direct answer."

"Did you and Kerris have an affair?"

"No, we didn't, but we kissed, and Cam walked in on it. I'm on my way to see her. Any other questions?"

"I wish I hadn't even called you. This is awful. No wonder Cam is bitter."

"I don't know what you want me to say." Walsh's words scissored into hers. "I can't undo what happened."

"Walsh, maybe you should just—"

"I'll be back in New York soon, and everyone will be happy."

Walsh wasn't sure if either of them believed the words, but that was where he left it.

Once at the hospital, Walsh eased the door open, holding his breath and stepping quietly into the room. Meredith's warning still rang in his head. It would be best for him and Cam not to run into each other. He just hoped Kerris would wake up before he needed to leave.

He settled down in the hard plastic chair, his eyes never leaving the small, embattled figure so still against the sheets. The facial scratches and scrapes, though still evident, were healing, and the bruising wasn't as prominent.

"Walsh." Kerris mumbled his name, twisting her head a little fitfully on the pillow.

Shocked by what he'd just heard, Walsh leaned forward, reaching for her hand, squeezing gently.

"Hey, sweetheart." He met her dazed eyes with a smile. "I'm here."

"Walsh?" Kerris's frown pulled at the scratches on her forehead. "What are you...are you..."

"You were asleep and called my name." He hoped he'd disguised how much satisfaction that brought him. "Is it okay that I'm here?"

Her eyes drifted over his shoulder to the open door, returning back to his watchful stare.

"Cam knows I'm here." Walsh answered her silent question, continuing when she raised her eyebrows in surprise. "Well, kind of. We had our run-in before you gained consciousness. He knows I'm in town and not leaving until you're out of the woods."

She shot him a look sprinkled with reproach.

"What?" He released the hand he was still holding, leaning back to settle in the chair. "What do you expect me to do?"

"Act normal?" Her smile was as teasing and affectionate as he could expect considering she was wired up à la Frankenstein.

"Normal's never worked for me."

He held her smile for as long as he could before sobering. She had provided the appropriate responses, but something was missing. A spark. A vibrancy. And it wasn't just the plastered arm and leg and wrapped ribs. There was something…vacant in her eyes. Then he remembered. He stroked her hand and touched the wooden bracelet Iyani had given her. The one that matched his own.

"I'm sorry about the baby."

She looked back at him, her composure wilting around the edges until it disappeared all together, leaving tears like standing water in her eyes.

"I don't know what else to say, so I'll just leave it at that." He refused to look away from her naked pain. She hadn't flinched at his when his mother died. "I'm sorry, baby."

Chapter Eight

*B*aby. *He'd called her baby.*

At Walsh's endearment, the tears Kerris had checked welled over, the salty wetness stinging her face where angry scratches remained. She swiped at the tears, dismayed when still more leaked out, refusing to be dammed. After months of feeling the baby—a girl, she had found out—move around inside, she felt so alone with her empty womb.

Walsh strode over to the door and turned the lock. He crossed back to the bed, shocking her when he carefully climbed up beside her unplastered right side and slipped his arm beneath her. It was the most awkward, uncomfortable…tender and cathartic embrace she had experienced since that night in the gazebo when he'd baptized her in her own tears. She'd shared the tragedy of her past with him, of how TJ had violated her. Walsh had called her a miracle, healing places she'd thought beyond anyone's touch.

She leaned her head into his strong shoulder, startled by the sound of her own wrenching sob. Her fingers clutched the sleeve of his shirt in a desperate claw. She burrowed into him, feeling some measure of peace for the first time since she'd opened her eyes to the debris of her life.

This should have been Cam sharing her pain, reaching in to soothe her heartache. She knew it, but couldn't bring herself to pull away from the man who seemed to always provide the perfect solace. Cam had slipped into the room earlier that morning and she had pretended to be asleep. He had stood silently over her, his guilt, his anger, his resentment, almost palpable. She had breathed it in, feeling it course through her barren soul, leaving a noxious trail in its wake. So her eyes had remained closed in a cowardly game of opossum.

"We didn't know it was a girl," she said into the silence Walsh's comfort had allowed her. "We hadn't even chosen a name."

"You hadn't thought of anything?"

"Well, I thought…maybe after Cam if it was a boy, and if it was a girl…"

"If it was a girl…"

"Amalie."

Walsh leaned back to glance down at her, a small smile settling on his face.

"That's beautiful."

"Different, huh?" Her voice broke in half on the words.

"Perfect."

"Did they…um, do you know if they put a name on the death certificate? Or the grave or anything?" She held her breath, waiting to hear the name her little girl had carried with her to the other side.

"No, you were still out, and I think they've left it blank." He frowned. "You and Cam haven't talked about any of this? I know only because Meredith mentioned it."

"We, um, haven't spoken." She squeezed the bridge of her nose. Even that ached, along with every other part of her wrecked body. "He came this morning, but I was asleep."

"Oh."

Walsh packed so much into that small word, and she ignored every bit of it. He was the last person with whom Kerris could discuss her marital problems. She leaned her throbbing head heavier against his shoulder.

"I don't want to be here."

"In the hospital? You may be going home next week."

"Not the hospital." She fiddled with the matching bracelet encircling his broad wrist. "Here. Alive."

"Don't say that." He grabbed her trembling chin between his thumb and index finger, less gentle than she would have expected.

"It's true." She couldn't look at the harsh planes of his face. Fresh tears tracked down her cheeks. "I wish I'd broken to pieces against that tree."

She gave in to the tears, her shoulders shaking and despair rattling her chest with every choked cry. Walsh touched the hair she knew must be limp and dirty by now.

"Kerris, remember when I was kidnapped?"

"Of course." She sniffed, giving up on any dignity in these most intimate moments. "It was awful."

"How would you have felt if I had died in Haiti?"

It would have gutted her. She would not have been able to hide her devastation from Cam or Jo or Kristeene or anyone who might have been around when she received that news. She would have collapsed and wept like a widow. She shook her head from side to side, her eyes locked on his.

"Yeah, that's what I would have felt if you hadn't made it. Worse."

"Walsh—"

"No, you listen to me." He planted a beam of steel in his words. "It was me in that chapel last week begging God to spare you. And it would've been me who would have died inside if you hadn't made it. So don't tell me you wish you weren't here."

"It's so hard." She didn't mean to moan, but the hurt had to escape somehow. "I don't think I can do it."

"You have a long road ahead of you. Some rehab and some hard days. Maybe some counseling? If you don't want to do this, it'll be that much harder."

"I know, I just…" Her voice trailed off on a hiccup, tears clogging her throat.

"Kerris, at my mom's funeral, I let you go. I did the right thing. You were pregnant. You were Cam's."

Kerris gulped, hoping he wasn't about to go there. She didn't have the strength.

"I don't have that resolve anymore. Not like I did." She felt his lips in her hair. "I came too close to losing you for good, and I can't promise to always let you go."

He let his head fall back beside hers against the pillow, giving her a sideways glance full of things that frightened her.

"Hearing you say these things, I can't leave you like this."

She tried to ease away a little, as much as the limited motion her two casts and the bindings around her ribs would allow.

"Walsh, you have to."

"You have to promise to try. If I even hear from Mama Jess that you're not trying, I'll be back. Don't test me. I'll come back and take care of you myself."

"Walsh, you don't have to do that. You can't do that."

"And am I supposed to trust Cam to do it?" The molten anger she realized he'd been carefully hiding from her slid under the shield guarding his composure.

"Walsh, he *will* take care of me."

"He needs to do a damn better job of it." The brambles in his voice scraped across her nerve endings. The anger he didn't bother to hide made his big body hard and unforgiving. She was cuddling a stone wall.

"And maybe I need to do a better job taking care of him." Kerris ran a finger along her hospital ID bracelet. "Maybe I need to be a better wife."

"What's that supposed to mean?"

He nudged her when she didn't respond.

"Nothing."

She refused to reveal what she knew Cam would see as the ultimate humiliation: the fact that she had called Walsh's name in her sleep. The guilt of that ate away at her.

"You'd better go," she said after they'd lain there huddled together for a few more moments, words unnecessary.

"I don't want to go." His lips brushed her ear with the words.

And I want you to stay forever, she thought, wondering if the pain in her torso was a broken rib or a broken heart.

"Please go." She denied herself the stolen pleasure of leaning up to kiss the hard line of his jaw.

The door closed behind him a few seconds later, and she swallowed her heart's rebel wail.

Please stay.

Chapter Nine

A breeze surprised Kerris in the stifling August heat, persuading a rare smile to her lips. There had been so little to smile about lately. She'd been home from the hospital for two weeks, and still had a lot of pain. The doctors said that was to be expected, since she had basically been body slammed by a tree. They had pills for the pain, and she took them, eager for numbness. But the pain under her skin? Slamming against the walls of her empty womb? Echoing in the hollow chambers of her heart? There was no pill for that. If there were, she would have overdosed on it by now.

She was lucky to be alive. But she sat on the patio on a gorgeous day, watching her gorgeous husband set lunch out for them, and felt anything but lucky. Cam maneuvered her wheelchair so her leg in its cast cleared the table.

"Good thing Mama Jess has cooked and frozen enough food

to feed the troops." He settled into the seat across from her, his smile artificial and forced.

Kerris carved out a smile for him.

"Yeah, Mama Jess has been a godsend."

She'd been coming over every day to help. Those times were the closest to peace Kerris had known for the last two weeks. When it was just Kerris and Cam, things were so awkward. Cam seemed as relieved as Kerris every time Mama Jess showed up. Faking it was exhausting. Sometimes Kerris took the pills just to be asleep whenever Cam was home.

He was trying. She was, too, but everything—every smile, every word, every look between them—was so hard. She thought longingly of the ease they had shared before they married, before they even dated. That pure, open friendship. They were both knotted souls under it all, but they'd shared a simple connection, built around honesty and mutual affection. She strained her eyes every day to see a trace of those friends, but all she could see was the wary distrust between them. All she could feel was the guilt they shared over Amalie's death.

He had looked at her with no expression when she told him the name she wanted for their baby girl. He nodded wordlessly, looking away from her searching eyes. Had he cried over the baby she'd never even gotten to hold? Did it feel like someone was shoving gravel into the soft muscle of his heart when he thought of Amalie, never having a chance?

Cam toyed with his napkin. He picked up his fork and then put it down. He looked to the left and watched the river, still and placid. He looked to the right, considering the vegetable garden she and Mama Jess had planted earlier in the summer. Even when her pregnancy had made it harder, Kerris had wandered out between those rows every day to check on her small patch of earth, pregnant with life, just like she had been.

Cam bullied the vegetables on his plate into corners, poking at them. He looked everywhere but at her. Kerris knew things had been difficult between them; she knew that they hadn't talked and needed to, but his restlessness disturbed her. He was like a wild boar penned and desperate to escape.

"Is everything okay, Cam?"

His broad shoulders slumped; his lean body was taut with an emotion he could barely disguise any longer. He looked at her, his face already telling her things she didn't want to know.

"Not for a long time, Kerris."

Amazing how words so softly spoken could feel like a spike splitting your heart.

"I don't understand."

Only she did understand, but had no idea what he wanted to do about it. His eyes skittered away, paying more attention to the patio flagstones than to his wife.

"Ker, I can't do this."

"You mean the rehab and everything?" She hoped that's what he meant. Something she had an easy, quick solution for. "That won't start 'til these casts are off. So we've got a while, and it won't be so bad. The nurse will be here during the day, and she'll take me to rehab. It won't interfere with work or anything. We'll get into a groove and—"

"Not the rehab. I can't do…us anymore. These last two weeks have been…The night of the accident, I said I was done." He finally looked her right in the eye, and the resolve she saw there shook her. "I still am."

So this was what it meant to feel the earth move under your feet; to feel the whole world tilt, and when it righted itself, for it to look like completely unfamiliar terrain. But not so unfamiliar. Really, ground she had covered all her life. Abandonment. Rejection. It actually felt strangely, sadly familiar. And she realized something in that moment. Though Cam had said he'd never let her go, she had been the one clinging with a grasping, desperate need she hadn't even acknowledged to herself. Finally, someone had committed to her. Someone had thought she was good enough, wanted her enough to make a permanent commitment. And she would have allowed nothing, not even the love of her life, to jeopardize that commitment.

"Say something." Cam's eyes under his long, thick lashes looked like he didn't know what to expect.

She sometimes forgot how beautiful Cam was. A dark angel. Even as she had held on to the mangled matrimonial ties that bound them, she had taken him for granted. She hadn't appreciated his kindness. Hadn't longed for the passion she knew he deliberately checked so he wouldn't frighten her. Hadn't sought out the secrets and the shadows behind his eyes.

Her throat blazed with the tears she refused to shed until she was alone.

"I am sorry, Cam."

"*You're* sorry?" Disbelief warred with guilt on his face. "Kerris, I almost got you killed. Our baby girl…"

His words and something in his eyes died. Maybe it was the last of his love for her. Maybe it was the dream of a family that had compelled every misbegotten step they had taken over the years. Maybe it was something he'd buried with Amalie.

"Cam, you are not responsible. If it's anyone's fault, it's mine. No one forced me behind that wheel."

"God, Kerris, don't make this easier for me." He cleared what she thought might be tears from his throat. "There's nothing you can say to make me feel like less of a bastard right now."

"I don't blame you," Kerris said. "It occurs to me sometimes to blame you, but deep down, I don't. And I guess eventually I'll have to get over blaming myself, but I'm not there yet."

"I thought we could make this work. But Amalie on top of what happened with…I kept telling myself we could get past it." Regret darkened his stormy eyes. "And I'm sorry for that night, for what I made you do. It was just the thought of you and Walsh—"

"Don't."

She had to stop him. She couldn't talk about the night he'd demanded her body as punishment for her sins. And Walsh's name between them was too much.

"Let's not dissect all the ways we hurt each other, Cam. Not today. I'm too…"

Too weary. Too injured, inside and out. Too desperate to be alone.

"Until the divorce is final, you're still on my insurance, so your medical bills should be covered." He stood, suddenly businesslike and brusque, but that didn't hide the desperation underneath. "I'm leaving tonight, so you can stay here for as long as you need to. Hell, you can have the cottage in the…in the settlement. You made it a home, and I know how much it means to you."

"Where will you stay?" She studied her cast, where Meredith and Mama Jess and a few nurses had signed it.

"I'm leaving tonight for Paris."

Her eyes shot to his face, shock and confusion competing for mastery in her muddled emotions.

"Paris?"

"I applied to the Sorbonne months ago and was accepted." He shuffled his feet, a dance of discomfort with himself. "I hadn't told you because I knew that would be shit hitting the fan on top of everything else we had going on. I delayed admission and was planning to talk to you about it after…after the baby was born."

"You mean you planned to spring it on me as a done deal, knowing I would cave and follow you over there."

"Yeah, that about says it all." Self-contempt twisted his well-shaped mouth around the admission. "But there's nothing here for me. Ms. Kris is gone. Walsh and I are done, obviously. Our marriage is a joke, maybe was from the beginning. Amalie is…"

Cam bit off the sentence as if the name had pierced his tongue. He titled his head back and looked up at the sky before returning to the conversation.

"Even though it's off term, Sebastian has some friends I can crash with until the next term begins. I'll get you the address once I settle in Paris."

"What about your job?"

"I quit my job a couple of weeks ago. Not like I really need it now that Ms. Kris's estate has settled. Meredith didn't tell you?"

"Meredith!" Her turbulent emotions exploded through the numbness his announcement had caused. "Why would *Meredith* have to tell me my husband quit his job?"

"Why would my *wife* pretend she was asleep every time I came to the hospital?" Cam returned with re-emerging fire.

They stared at each other, helpless and hostile, a suffocating silence stealing their breaths.

"I didn't know what to say to you." Her voice abandoned the fight, leaving behind a whisper. A rogue tear slipped down her cheek at the memory of him standing over her in the hospital. "And I assumed you didn't know what to say to me."

"I didn't. I figured Walsh had said it all."

His acrid words slapped her, and she shut her eyes against the stinging reproach.

"You think I didn't know he came to see you? That he was getting a play by play from Meredith?"

"He only came once, and I don't think he tried to hide it."

"No, I've never met a man as bold as Walsh about stealing another man's wife."

"He was concerned about me. We're friends."

"Fuck!" He detonated the imprecation like a bomb, pulling the ring on the tenuous control she'd sensed him exerting. "Even now you can't admit that you love him? That's what this is all about. That's why we didn't work. If he had just...if you could have..."

A groan escaped the bear trap of Cam's tightly clenched lips. He pulled a hand over his face before running it along the back of his neck.

"Fuck." He inflated the expletive with frustration and hurt. He turned his head away, wiping surreptitiously at the wet corners of his eyes. He moved toward the patio door, cocking his ear, listening for something she didn't hear.

"Expecting someone?" She felt listless beneath the weight of the tragedy they had become.

"Um, yeah." He walked to the door leading back inside. "Meredith's dropping off Mama Jess."

"What for?" She imagined Mama Jess walking into this minefield they were negotiating right now. She would pick up on it right away. "She can come back later. We should finish this."

"That's what I'm telling you." Cam headed toward the door and looked at her over his shoulder. "It *is* finished. I'm leaving, and Mama Jess is staying with you."

"That's ridiculous." She used her good hand to bang her good leg in the wheelchair. "I'll be fine. We can't expect her to drop everything and just...just..."

She trailed off when Mama Jess came to the patio door. All of Kerris's arguments and reasons why Mama Jess shouldn't come, shouldn't drop everything to be with her, disintegrated. She realized it was exactly what she wanted, exactly what she needed to get through this. What she'd never had. A mother who would drop it all, do it all, fight it all, for her little girl. And that was how Mama Jess looked at her in that moment: like she was a tigress and Kerris her cub.

"You," Mama Jess practically growled at Cam, "can go now."

"Mama Jess, I was just—"

"Whatever you were *just* doing, you can *just* do it in Paris or wherever you're flying off to. Go. We got this."

"My flight doesn't actually leave until eight." Cam walked over and squatted down in front of the wheelchair. He took Kerris's hand despite the small rumble coming from Mama Jess.

"I know…shit. I know everything's screwed up," Cam said. "I just…I can't stay here. We can't keep pretending it'll get better. You understand?"

She looked down at his thundercloud eyes in his angel face. Their marriage was a decomposing body, its rotting fetor of betrayal and mistrust clogging the air between them, but she knew he still cared. Whatever part of him still loved her was being ripped out by this end. She could see it. She knew it, but her heart still beat a painful cadence.

Abandoned. Rejected. Walked out on again.

The ties that bound them, though mangled and matted, Cam was the one severing.

"I understand." Kerris hoped he wasn't distracted by the tears she couldn't keep from rolling down her cheeks. "Go. I get it."

"Yeah, well, uh…"

Cam tipped his head back, probably searching for words

that would make something right that had been wrong from the beginning. His throat worked around his Adam's apple, one tear tracking into the dark silk of his hairline. She swiped at his tear with her thumb, lifting one heavy corner of her mouth.

"It's all right, Cam," she whispered, glad Mama Jess had gone back inside. "Just go."

"Kerris, I do love—"

"Don't say it." She cut him off, a please-get-out-of-here-before-I-break plea in her eyes. His voice was a dull-edged knife slicing clumsily through her heart, fiber by bloody fiber. Dull and slow and imprecise and drawn out. She would have preferred a quick cut, but he just kept talking.

"If you need anything…"

"Go. Thank you for getting Mama Jess to stay here with me. She's exactly what I need."

"Will you…" Cam swallowed, pressing his lips together. "Will you be with him now?"

The question dangled between them. She oscillated between flaring, blazing emotion, and a telling numbness that permeated her bones to the very marrow. She was an open wound, vulnerable and infected. She had been through a lot, and the most dangerous thing she could do now was to decide. She was afraid to move, afraid she'd screw things up even worse than she had already.

Still. She needed to be still.

She shrugged shoulders that felt like they couldn't have cared less. She stroked Iyani's bracelet on her wrist.

"I really don't know. Not now, not anytime soon. I'm afraid to be with anyone right now. When you leave, I'll truly be alone. And I think that's what I need."

"Well, if you need me, you know where I am."

He stood up and walked inside, leaving Kerris with just the breeze for company. She knew he would not hear from her and she would not hear from him. She almost forgot to hurt when the door closed behind him. It was now such a familiar sound.

Chapter Ten

Walsh stuffed the last few items into his bag, giving his bedroom a cursory inspection before heading toward the stairs. His flight didn't leave for another three hours, but he had to get out of this house. It didn't feel like home anymore. He'd remained in Rivermont longer than he had planned. Jo and the board of directors had drawn him into foundation issues he hadn't had time for over the last year or so. Uncle James had gotten in last night from his business trip. They'd knocked back a few brews and watched whatever was on ESPN. Their relationship was as vital and essential as ever, but things weren't quite the same between Walsh and Jo.

The kiss he'd shared with Kerris had been an earthquake, splintering his most important friendship. Unfortunately, he'd felt the aftershocks in his relationship with Jo. They hadn't spoken much since her visit to New York, and he knew she didn't approve of his being here now for Kerris. The strained, frozen silence between them belied the years of warmth and laughter they'd shared in this very house.

Each summer he, Jo, and Cam had raced through the backyard, flown down to the river, and raised hell in the halls of this place his mother had made feel like home. Only one thing hurt almost as much as losing Kerris, and that was losing Cam and Jo.

As if the force of his thoughts had conjured them up, he heard their voices at the bottom of the stairs.

"You're leaving?" Jo's voice carried up the staircase. "But where? When?"

"I'm going to Paris." Walsh heard the barely suppressed excitement in Cam's voice. "My flight leaves at eight."

"The Sorbonne? You told her?"

"Yeah, and I…Jo, I told her I want a divorce."

Walsh leaned against the wall, afraid his weak knees wouldn't support him. His heart battered his chest, straining against the wall of bone and muscle. Hot air panted over his dry lips, his breath shallowing at the thought of Kerris being free. Of having her. Then he recalled how she'd looked the last time he'd seen her, how he'd had to force himself to leave her there in that hospital bed, cheeks still wet from tears she'd shed over Amalie. He pushed away from the wall, rounding the stairs and storming down them until he stood in front of Cam. Walsh dropped his bags to the floor and gave Cam an unwavering glare.

"Going somewhere?"

"None of your business," Cam shot back.

"You son of a bitch." Walsh grabbed a fistful of Cam's shirt and dragged him close enough to hit. "You're leaving her? *Now?*"

Cam shoved, putting as much distance between him and Walsh as the death grip on his shirt would allow.

"I'm the son of a bitch?" The calm in Cam's voice would have fooled some, but not Walsh. "I'm getting out 'cause I didn't sign up for a ménage à trois. If you wanna blame anyone for this, blame yourself. I do."

Walsh slowly released the fabric clutched in his hands, watching the smooth mask of Cam's face.

"You're going to Paris? You're divorcing her?"

"Yeah. At least wait until I'm on the plane before you rush over there."

"You left her alone? With all she has to go through?"

"I would never do that, but there's no need for me to stay. Mama Jess moved in to take care of her." Cam looked down at his shoes. "Thought you'd be happy."

"It's not the way I wanted...I'm sorry, Cam."

Cam looked up, narrowing his eyes and lacing his words with sarcasm.

"Sorry? Jo, he's sorry. You screw up my marriage, my only shot at a family of my own, and you're *sorry*? Wow. Your mom would be so proud."

"Shut the hell up." Menace and anger tightened Walsh's face. His fists balled at his side. "Don't even say her name."

"That's how Ms. Kris raised you?" Cam dug around in Walsh's wound, heedless of the growing violence Walsh felt in his chest and knew must be all over his face. "Just like your daddy. No respect for marriage vows."

"Cam, I'm warning you."

Walsh willed back the flame rising up his neck. He licked his top lip, finding it wet with the sweat of his anger and agitation.

"It's okay." A bitter smile marred Cam's face. "You got the girl, like you get everything else. Just remember. That's my leftovers. I broke her in for you."

Bone slammed into bone when Walsh's fist connected with Cam's jaw. And then they were on the floor, writhing on the cold tiles of the foyer. Walsh sat on Cam's chest, pounding his fist into his face, mindless in his rage. Cam managed to reach up, even from that awkward angle, landing several punches to Walsh's eye and chin. They didn't talk. There was nothing left to say. The only sounds in the foyer were the grunts, the punches—the sounds of a violent confrontation long overdue.

Surreal. It couldn't be happening. This wasn't Walsh's best friend, his brother, whose nose gushed blood under the relentless anvil of his fist. Even the blood pouring from a gash above Walsh's eye wasn't real; it wasn't enough to wrest him from the nightmare of friendship slaughtered in the very house where they had played.

"Daddy!" Jo screamed, running toward Uncle James's study.

Unc rounded the corner, his glasses resting low on his nose, the document he'd been studying still in his hand.

"What the hell! Break it up!"

Uncle James plunged into the merciless battle between the two men. He pulled at Walsh's shoulders, trying to dislodge him. He grabbed Walsh's arm before his fist could connect again with Cam's face.

Cam dragged himself to sit against the wall, elbows resting on the knees he pulled up. He offered a maniacal grin, blood lacing his teeth and running down his chin.

"You're such a spoiled bastard," he spat at Walsh, the look he leveled at him malevolent.

Cam gestured to the stately foyer.

"You've had everything since the day you were born. All this. The best schools, great family. A mother…"

Cam's voice broke. He closed his eyes and shook his head, wiping at the blood on his face.

"And you just had to have my girl."

"It wasn't like that." Walsh heaved precious air through his lungs, spent from their violent exertion. He stretched out on the floor, looking up at the crystal chandelier overhead. "We didn't...we never—"

"Just because you never fucked her—"

"Cam, good grief," Uncle James said. "That's your wife."

"Oh, you didn't hear?" Cam dragged himself to his feet. "She's not my wife anymore. At least not for long."

"What's he talking about, Walsh?" Unc asked.

Walsh couldn't meet the disapproval and disappointment in his uncle's eyes.

He remained silent, banging his head once against the floor. He felt like an insect Cam had stretched out beneath a magnifying glass, three sets of eyes singeing him with unrelenting sun rays. They all watched him with varying degrees of censure and judgment.

"Oh, nothing to say now?" Cam swiped at his still-bleeding nose with the hem of his shirt. "Let's just say that Walsh and Kerris had a...special relationship that didn't leave much room for her husband."

Walsh gulped back the shame boiling up in his throat, never taking his eyes from the glittering light fixture above. His faulty character was on display here in the house where his mother had raised him, where Uncle James had taught him to be a man.

Walsh forced himself to sit up and face Cam.

"I don't know what to say other than I'm sorry."

"Is it true?" Uncle James, face a blank sheet of paper with just a few lines, waited for Walsh's response.

Walsh looked at his uncle, unable to apologize.

"I love her. I loved her before Cam even married her."

Walsh turned his eyes to Cam, who looked back at him like an enemy.

"What I regret is not telling you, Cam. Thinking I could handle it. Thinking it would go away. The kiss you walked in on should never have happened."

"Jesus, Walsh." Uncle James's disillusionment whooshed from his mouth in one quick breath. He ran his hand over his face. "How could you?"

"What? Kiss her?" Walsh stood to his feet. "One kiss. If it had been up to me, she would have left your ass a long time ago, Cam. That would never have happened, though. And you know why? Because that's the kind of woman you married."

Cam looked back at Walsh, unblinking and silent.

"She would never have left you for me. Never have cheated on you. One kiss, and you're throwing that away?"

"A lifetime with a woman who loves someone else?" Cam twisted his eyebrows into a frown. "Would you take that?"

"I'd take Kerris any way I could get her." Walsh cleared his face of repentance or apology. He grabbed his bags from where he'd dropped them. "As a matter of fact, I'll take her as your...how did you put it? Broken-in leftovers? Yeah, I'd take her if she'd had *seven* husbands, not just one idiot ahead of me."

"So you're really going after her?" Cam asked.

Walsh walked to the door and knew this would be it. This would be final.

"Unc, would you run me to the airport?" Walsh looked past Cam and Jo to where his uncle stood. "I'll wait in the car."

Chapter Eleven

Mama Jess, I need you to do me a favor."

Kerris glanced from the bulk of her two casts, lumps beneath the comforter, up to Mama Jess's worried face. She had cried for only a few minutes after Cam left, and then she'd retreated to her office on the screened-in porch. From her wheelchair by the window, she'd looked out and down to the riverbank. Mama Jess had finally convinced her to eat some soup and a sandwich. A quiet meal, with Mama Jess not asking many questions, and Kerris not offering many remarks. After eating just a few spoonfuls of soup and pulling the crusts from her sandwich, Kerris had declared herself exhausted and in need of a nap. And now she was in need of a favor as well.

"What is it, Lil' Bit?" Mama Jess reached down to push the bangs from Kerris's eyes.

"When Walsh comes." She caught Mama Jess's hand by her face, gripping her fingers. "I don't want to see him."

"Do you know that he'll come?"

"He'll come." Kerris licked dry lips. "I just don't...I can't see him."

"I saw him crying his heart out in the chapel." Mama Jess adjusted the comforter around Kerris's shoulder, looking down at her with eyes blessedly free of judgment. "That man loves you."

"I know, and I care..." Kerris let the insipid word describing what she felt for Walsh sit on her tongue like tasteless porridge. "I care about him, which is why I can't see him right now."

"Mind explaining that?"

"There's something broken in me. Something that's never been right. I used Cam to try to fix it. I used the baby to try to fix it. And if Walsh comes now, as much as I...care about him, I'll use him to try to fix it, too."

"Hmmmm." Mama Jess crammed everything and nothing into that monosyllable.

"And I can't do that," Kerris said, her eyes filling up. "Not anymore. Not to *him*. I need to be on my own and figure this out. And if he comes...I won't be able to say no. I won't be able to send him away. And I just...I just need some time to get it straight. To sort it out. I've messed up so badly, and I can't keep—"

"Stop, baby." Mama Jess's voice, quiet and sharp, sliced into the hysterical note Kerris heard building in her own voice. "I'll handle it."

* * *

Walsh pressed the doorbell again for the fourth time in a matter of seconds. Cam said Mama Jess was here with Kerris. Walsh walked over to the window, trying to see through the sheers into the living room. He knocked on the window, a few soft taps. Maybe he should go around to the back door. Maybe he'd knocked too softly, and the steady rainfall had muffled the sound. He put a little more insistence into the fist he banged against the windowpane. It shouldn't take this long to open a door. Surely Mama Jess hadn't left Kerris here alone.

The front door opened before he could send his anxious mind too far down that road.

Mama Jess stepped onto the front porch, closing the door behind her and leaning against it.

"Were you going to call the fire department next?"

Mama Jess started her scrupulous inspection at his shoes, then inched up his dark-wash jeans and past his NYU T-shirt until she met his eyes. Walsh didn't like what he saw there. It was steel. It was determination. The fact that she didn't let him in hadn't escaped him. Walsh walked the few feet from the window to the front door, standing his ground in front of the woman he suspected meant to keep him out.

"I'm here to see Kerris."

"Oh, and here I was about to get flattered." She rolled the words around in sarcasm and accompanied them with a twist of her lips.

"I…well, I heard that—"

"News sure travels fast." She squinted up at him in the weak porch light and gestured to his face. "What's the other guy look like?"

Walsh touched the puffiness under one eye and brushed his fingers across the cut above the other.

"Worse." Walsh shoved all thought of Cam from his mind. He had waited too long. This was happening. Tonight. Now. "I need to see Kerris."

"No." Her lips barely parted over the word, like it was nothing to her either way, but Walsh wasn't fooled.

"Is she asleep? My flight leaves in a couple of hours, but I can wait. I could even reschedule my flight. Cancel it. I can stay another day. Another week. I just need to see her."

"Even when she wakes up, she don't want to see you, son." Mama Jess's firm tone gentled just a little over the last part, but that brought Walsh little comfort.

"No, she will." Walsh tried the usual confident smile, but it slipped and fell right off his face when he saw just how unmoved Mama Jess remained. "She'll want to see me."

"Then why did she tell me that if you came by, to tell you she don't wanna see you?"

Walsh gave a vigorous shake of his head, denials fighting their way out of his mouth and tumbling past his lips.

"No, you must have misunderstood. She would never say that. Now that—"

"Now that she's getting a divorce?" Mama Jess pushed away from the door, planting a fist on one full hip. "And now she'll be free? Is that what you were gonna say?"

"Not exactly, but…can I just come in? Just for a few minutes."

"I said no. Now go."

"Go? You're telling me to go?"

"No, *she's* telling you to go. Look, give her some time." Mama Jess heaved her full bosom with a sigh that seemed to say she was barely tolerating him. "Don't be a spoiled little boy about it. Don't you have money to make, orphans to save, and things to do?"

"Spoiled?" Walsh knew he was in trouble when he started sputtering. "Wha…I…You…Me? Spoiled?"

"Look, all I know is you out here, banging on the door, pounding on the window, whining 'cause you can't get your way, and 'bout to pitch a fit 'cause I won't let you disturb a woman who barely survived a car wreck, lost her baby and was just walked out on by her husband." Mama Jess leaned forward and up until he couldn't escape the strength of her brown eyes. "*Excuse* her for needing a minute."

"I just need—"

"How about what she needs?"

God, he hoped Kerris needed him. As badly as he needed her. Desperation and desolation muddled Walsh's thoughts. He, who had persuaded sheikhs out of oil holdings in their families for generations, couldn't convince one middle-aged woman to let him into a cottage that had been in his own family for more than a hundred years? Nothing had worked, so all he had left was the truth.

"I can't lose her again." He said it so softly that the rain now coming down steadily almost drowned it out. "I waited once before. Tried to leave it up to her to fix things, and it got so messed up she married my best friend."

Walsh flinted the stare he leveled back at Mama Jess.

"I will *not* let that happen again. I don't care if you make me wait out here for a week."

Mama Jess's mouth softened, but she still didn't make a move to open the door.

"Let's make a deal." She gestured toward the porch swing. "Sit down."

Walsh remained rooted right where he stood. The swing was at least eight feet farther from the door than his current position.

"What kind of deal?"

Mama Jess smacked her lips together, impatience marking her smooth brown face.

"Boy, just sit down."

He settled on the wooden seat beside Mama Jess, pushing his back into the corner and keeping his eye on her. She reminded him of his mother. They were as physically dissimilar as two women could be, but Walsh knew wily when he saw it. He'd lived with it, been raised by it. Had loved it. Mama Jess's eyes held the same shrewdness his mother's had. He swallowed the hot lump in his throat and braced himself for terms he probably wouldn't like.

"I'll let you know when she's ready."

"I'm supposed to trust that you…that she—" He stopped, breathing through his nose and out through his mouth once, a huff of anxious air that deflated his chest. "Okay. You'll let me know if she's not healing right? If she needs anything? Financially, medically—anything?"

"She won't need anything."

"You will let me know." He bolstered the words with a stony glare that set terms of his own.

"I'll let you know. She does care about you, you know."

That was a crumb, a bone thrown, an insult to what he had with Kerris.

"She *cared* about me the day she married my best friend, so forgive me for not putting much stock in that." Walsh's bitterness and regret popped out like a jack-in-the-box. He tried to tuck them both neatly away before continuing in a more even voice. "Do we have a deal, or what?"

"And you won't contact her until I contact you?"

"This won't work."

"Walsh, you let her do the work on herself now, or sign up for a lifetime of trouble."

Walsh stiffened, his nervous movements slowing to nothing.

There was that word—that elusive word he'd never thought would ever apply to him and Kerris.

"Did you say 'a lifetime'?"

"If you play your cards right, maybe." Mama Jess rationed a tiny smile for the first time since he had banged on the door.

With just a nod and without another word, Walsh stood and walked down the porch steps toward the dark Mercedes idling in the driveway, his pace not rushed despite the rain pelting his head and shoulders. He'd forgotten Uncle James was even waiting. His tunnel vision had blocked that out. Blocked out the fight with Cam. Blocked out Jo's disapproval and disappointment. Single-mindedness had possessed him, but he came back to himself with every step he took away from the cottage and toward the car.

Kerris had months of rehab ahead of her, and probably needed some therapy for all she'd been through, Amalie and Cam notwithstanding. The road ahead of her for the foreseeable future was rough, and more than anything, Walsh wanted to walk it with her. But he got it. She needed to do this alone. He made a promise to himself, and even though she couldn't hear it, a promise to the girl behind that door. This would be the last time he walked away from her. After this, never again.

After this, she owed him a lifetime.

Chapter Twelve

Walsh stood on the steps of the *other* house where he had grown up. This one, a three-story townhome in TriBeCa, had stood empty since his parents' divorce. Walsh had loved growing up in New York City, just as much, if not more than, he'd loved growing up in Rivermont.

Martin came down the stairs and into the foyer to face Walsh.

"Thanks for coming, son."

Remembering what he was here for, Walsh reached inside his suit jacket pocket for the small bag he'd retrieved from Uncle James to pass on to his father.

"No, problem, Dad. From the estate." Walsh extended the bag, watching his father's features twist with pain before shuttering into the aloof mask he usually wore. "I was surprised you chose to meet here instead of the office."

"Well, I wanted to talk to you about a few other things."

Martin almost reluctantly took the bag. "And this seemed like the best place to do it."

Walsh considered the gleaming hardwood floors, the wide windows, the curving staircase. He had slid down that banister, much to his mother's horror.

"I haven't been here since…wow, since the divorce."

"Me either, very much. I'm at the apartment most of the time. I'm considering selling."

"Selling the house?" Walsh was surprised by the tight lurch of his stomach. "Why would you do that?"

"You just said it. You haven't been here since the divorce, and neither have I. The better question is why haven't I sold it yet."

Martin glanced at the bag in his hands, denting his forehead with a frown. He turned his back to Walsh, walking over to look out the window to the street, running his index finger along the silk rope holding the ends of the velvet bag closed. Martin shook his head, clearing his throat and turning to glance at Walsh.

"I fucked up, Walsh."

Walsh wanted to rush over and clamp his hand over his father's mouth, stopping him from going any further, even though he longed to hear what he would disclose.

"Your mother." Martin paused to swallow visibly. "Your mother was everything to me. I know you find that hard to believe considering that I…that I cheated on her, but she was. And I got so mixed up, so turned around. When I found out who her family was—and I know you won't believe me, but I really didn't know when we got married."

"I believe you." Walsh leaned against the wall, tracing a dent from one of his childhood misadventures.

"I worked my ass off. I had so much to prove, and all I ended up proving was what a dick I was."

Walsh wished he could protest; wished he could tell his father not to be so hard on himself, but he'd never forget the sound of his mother's sobs through these very walls. Walsh watched his father's fingers tremble over the ropes that would reveal his mother's final sentiments.

"You gonna open that?" Walsh asked. "I can, um, I can leave if you want some privacy."

"She died in my arms, you know." Martin ignored Walsh's offer, still contemplating the street.

Walsh didn't respond to his father's comment. The intimacy he'd witnessed from the confines of his mother's closet—those last moments in his father's arms—was too much to speak of. He watched mutely as his father reached into the bag, pulling out a small band of gold. Simple. Unassuming. Practically tarnished, and yet his father's hand shook as he held it.

"Shit," his father breathed, blinking rapidly against the tears gathering in his eyes. "She really turned the knife with this one."

Walsh hung back, feeling like such an intruder. He wanted to ask about the ring's significance; to find out why his father seemed so undone by it, but the words seized in his throat. His father raised the ring to his lips reverently.

"It's her wedding ring."

Walsh remembered his mother's ring as a huge diamond of at least a few carats, with an accompanying band of platinum. He was sure he'd never seen this one before.

"We basically eloped," his father went on, not waiting for Walsh's questions. "And I barely had a pot to piss in. This ring was fifty dollars. All she asked was that it not turn her finger green."

Martin chuckled, a sound that creaked in his throat.

"Thought your Grandma Walsh would pass out when she got a load of this ring." He gave a slow shake of his head. "I took one look at the ring on *her* finger and understood why. It was two years before I made my first million and got your mother the ring you probably remember. I hadn't seen this one...well, not since then. Can't believe she kept this cheap old thing."

His father's voice collapsed over the last word, a sob choking him. He laid his forehead against the windowpane, his face wreathed in tears. And Walsh understood. He knew what it felt like to believe the rest of your life stretched out in front of you like a barren land because the one you loved wouldn't share it with you. Like you had missed a window you hadn't known would close so soon, and would rue it all your life. Walsh promised himself he would not squander his second chance with Kerris.

"All those years." Martin wiped his nose with the back of his suit jacket sleeve. "I worked so hard to prove myself to her and her family, to get all the things I thought her family expected, and she kept this. Of all the—"

He broke off again, this time burying his face in his big hands, tears sliding between his fingers. Walsh was at a loss. This was only the second time in his entire life he had seen his father unraveled, his composure completely absent. His arrogant assurance vanquished by this inconsolable grief.

Walsh touched his shoulder lightly, testing. Martin stiffened, seeming to remember that he was not alone. He pulled his face out of his hands, swiping his cheeks and struggling for a composure he just couldn't seem to regain. His face crumpled again, his mouth opening on a soundless wail. Walsh wrapped his arms fully around his father, still prepared to straighten and pull away if necessary. But his father leaned against him, his tall, muscular frame shaking with the tears he could no longer hold back.

Martin finally pulled himself to his full height, peering at his son, searching his eyes. Was he looking for judgment? Any sign of lost respect? He wouldn't find it. If anything, Walsh had finally found something in his father truly worthy of his respect.

"I kept this house"—Martin shoved his hands into his pockets and paced back toward the window and the now nearly darkened street—"because I thought one day we'd live here again together."

Walsh almost laughed. Not from humor, but the dry, angry bark of a child needlessly cheated of so much. His parents had been stubborn, blind, and madly in love. And had never been able to get their shit together long enough to reconcile.

"You had a funny way of showing it," Walsh said before he could stop himself, hating the wince his words caused on his father's face. "I'm sorry, Dad."

"No, you're right. She had her charities and I had my business and we just let the years go by."

"Was that all?" Walsh's voice hardened without his consent. "You don't think it had anything to do with your infidelity?"

His father looked back at Walsh, a patina of shame coating his eyes.

"I guess I have to take credit for that. That thing in you that kicks when someone's down."

"I'm sorry." Walsh exhaled the anger that had dogged him for years whenever he was around his father. "I just wish things could have been different."

"No, you're right. It was only the one time, but she couldn't forgive me and I couldn't set my pride aside long enough to beg her to." Martin pulled the small bag back out, stroking the rope. "I have to live the rest of my life knowing I could have had your mother back, that she loved me and that I loved her, and we didn't try."

Martin rearranged his features with efficiency back into their customary impassivity.

"So, this house has to go. I just wanted you to know."

"It doesn't feel right." Walsh rubbed the toe of his shoe over a nick in the hardwood floor.

"From a purely business perspective, I'd get a massive return." Martin ran his eyes over the expensive paneling and the high ceilings. "When we moved here, TriBeCa hadn't exploded the way it has now. It's gone up, down, and back up again since we bought it."

"But it's not purely business. You held on to this house all these years, saving it for when Mom would come back. You just cried your eyes out over a fifty-dollar ring. I know your secret now, Dad. You're sentimental."

"Don't be fooled." Martin crooked his mouth to one side, shifting his legs into his buccaneer's stance. "I don't have much time for sentiment right now. I have to focus on wrapping up our friend the sheikh."

Walsh went on high alert at the mention of the account he'd abandoned to remain near Kerris after the accident.

"I thought Miller was sewing that up."

"He missed a stitch or two." A hint of contempt deepened Martin's voice. "That boy. He's brilliant, and hungry, but sometimes he's so busy measuring his own dick he misses the little things."

"His dick *is* a little thing." Walsh amused himself with his own crassness, and was surprised when his father laughed aloud, slapping him on the back.

"That's pretty good," Martin said, still smiling. "Look, I'll hold off on selling the house, and maybe you should come with me. You know Kassim better than all of us now, and he likes you. He asked me how your friend was doing last time I spoke to him. I didn't know you'd hijacked his jet to fly to Rivermont."

"Yeah, and in the middle of the night. Looking back, I can't believe my own balls on that one."

"Guess you get those from me, too." Martin's face was straight, but his eyes held a crooked twinkle.

Walsh laughed, trying to remember when he and his father had joked this much. Maybe never.

"So what do you say?" Martin persisted. "You coming to Saudi or what?"

"Why not?" Walsh shrugged one broad shoulder. "Beats moping around the city."

"What do you have to mope about?"

"Nothing, it's just…well, Cam and Kerris are getting a divorce."

"Seems like that would be cause for celebration." A puzzled frown sketched Martin's forehead.

"I don't feel much like celebrating since she won't see me." Walsh sat on a step of the staircase. "I'm giving her a year."

"A year? She's a beautiful girl. You think the men in Rivermont are blind, son?"

"Don't remind me." Walsh closed his eyes in now-familiar agony. "I keep imagining some bastard getting next to her while I sit back giving her 'space' like a neutered pet."

"So what gives? It's not like you to lay back."

"North Carolina requires a yearlong separation, but then the divorce will be processed pretty quickly." Walsh bounced his feet on the stair beneath him, allowing his own words to excite him. "She's been through a lot, not just recently, but a lifetime of crap. She wants time to work on herself. And I, like a lovesick idiot, am actually giving it to her. For the last month, her friend Mama

Jess has been updating me. If it weren't for her, I'd be down there screwing this all up."

"And you're sure waiting is the best course of action?"

"Right now, it's the only course of action," Walsh said through tight lips, leaning his elbows back on the step behind him. "But I feel like a bull at a rodeo, locked behind the fence."

"A bull, huh?" Martin laughed. "Don't let Kassim hear that. I'm sure he'd like to put you out to stud. If we go to Saudi Arabia, he'll have plenty of Arabian ass to flash at you."

"I don't want anyone else." Walsh was sure that his father, and just about every man he'd meet on the street, wouldn't understand. His father had loved his mother until the day she died, but Martin hadn't been celibate for the last fifteen years.

"And you're not frustrated?"

"Only for her." Walsh shifted with a little discomfort, aroused by the mere memory of Kerris. Her taste. Her scent. The feel of her pressed and yielding against him. "I'll wait a year."

"And after that?"

"I'll win her," Walsh said, his natural self-assurance asserting itself.

"And if she doesn't want to be 'won'?"

"Remember what you told me I'd have to do if Merrist didn't cooperate when we were negotiating that merger a while back?"

"Hostile takeover," his father said, grinning widely.

"Exactly."

Chapter Thirteen

Kerris glanced around the crowded hotel ballroom, decorated for the Walsh Foundation's Christmas party. She couldn't help but remember the last time she'd been in this room. She had been honored as Scholar of the Year that night. It seemed in some ways like yesterday, and in some ways like an entirely different lifetime, one in which she and Cam had been little more than friends and not quite lovers, unsuspecting of the beautiful bomb poised to drop in the middle of their little idyll.

Walsh.

She had met Walsh here. She'd thought of him as a mountain that night—physically imposing and with more presence than she'd ever encountered in one man. She'd thought him a prince, and she had been right. Her chest tightened as her mind sketched her last impression of him four months ago, stretched out so carefully and taking up most of the hospital bed. Holding her as closely as he dared with her so injured, absorbing her tears and her pain like a loving sponge. It had taken all of her willpower not to call him when Mama Jess confirmed that he had indeed come, as she had known he would.

She never allowed her mind to stray much further than the next day. That's how she'd gotten through those first miserable weeks without Cam and without Walsh, an arm and a leg plastered, and her heart like broken glass, myriad and shattered. That's how she'd gotten through two months of rehab once the casts were off. That's how she got through every morning she woke up, wondering what Amalie would be doing by now.

This would have been her baby's first Christmas. Kerris had always imagined decorating a home for the holidays. A home filled with children, gingerbread, collard greens, and mistletoe and every tradition she could cram into the holiday season.

Kerris always manned a face painting and crafts table for the kids for the holiday event. She grinned, wondering how many reindeer and Santa Claus faces she'd paint before the night was over.

An hour later, Kerris was finishing a Rudolph nose on a little brown-faced cherub when she sensed someone standing nearby. She looked up, the ready smile on her face freezing when her eyes met Jo's. She looked just beyond Jo's shoulder, hoping to see at least one child waiting, but unfortunately there was a lull. Kerris dropped a quick kiss on the little girl's painted cheek before sending her on her way.

"Jo, hi." Kerris wiped the last traces of paint from her hands. "How are you?"

"I'm good. I didn't know you'd be here tonight."

"Haven't missed one since junior year."

"Yeah, I know."

Kerris searched for neutral things they could discuss. Things that didn't involve Walsh or Cam.

"Thanks for getting the clothes to us."

Ms. Kris had left Déjà Vu more than half her expansive wardrobe. Jo had handed over each item like it was a treasure. Meredith had "curated" all the clothes, which were so much finer than anything else the shop carried.

"No problem." Jo grinned and gave a subtle shake of her head. "That Meredith is something else."

Meredith and Jo had actually become friends through the process. The incongruity of that friendship made Kerris smile.

Jo plunged into the silence Kerris wasn't sure how to fill.

"It's the first Christmas without Aunt Kris. Can't believe she's been gone almost a year now." Jo looked around the brightly decorated room. "It's been tough."

"I'm sure. I miss her, and I can only imagine how hard it's been for the family."

Jo's hair had grown out of the sharp bob she typically maintained. As regal as ever, she looked even more like Kristeene with the softer hairstyle. Kerris hoped Jo would discover as much of Kristeene's likeness inside as she wore on her lovely face and tall, lithe body.

"Daddy and I don't even want to be in the house for Christmas." Jo twisted a ring on her middle finger that Kerris recognized as one Kristeene had often worn. "Thanksgiving was...well, it just wasn't the same. I think we're going to Kenya for Christmas with Walsh and Uncle Martin."

"Your Uncle Martin is going to Kenya for Christmas?" Kerris didn't even try to hide her surprise.

"If you can believe it, he and Walsh have been globetrotting together." Jo shook her head, a wry smile tweaking her full mouth.

"They've spent the last few months in Saudi Arabia and Hong Kong. It's probably the most time they've spent together in...well, ever. And somehow Walsh convinced Uncle Martin to spend Christmas with him at our Kenyan orphanage."

"That's great." Kerris shifted on the stool she'd been glued to for the last hour. "I like Mr. Bennett."

"You are definitely in the minority." Jo hesitated before pulling up one of the small red chairs the kids had been sitting in. "What exactly did you like about him?"

"That he brought Walsh home when no one else could." Kerris braced herself for the judgment she anticipated in Jo's eyes.

Jo looked back at her, the easy smile disappearing.

"Have you spoken to Walsh?" Jo toyed with a small pot of glitter, her tone neutral.

"No, not at all." Kerris rose to straighten her paints and crafts materials, afraid of where this could take them.

"What about Cam?"

Kerris's movements slowed until she stood completely still. She studied her hands, poised over the craft debris, noting the paler band of skin where her wedding ring had rested.

"No, not at all." Kerris's voice pitched low, diving with her heart at the thought of her last conversation with Cam. "Have you?"

"We talk every couple of weeks. He's doing well. Loves Paris. Loves the Sorbonne."

"He deserves this shot." Kerris forced herself to move again, swiping a pile of glitter into her cupped palm and then into the trash. "He's a brilliant artist."

"Always has been. I'm sorry things didn't work out for you two."

Kerris raised frank eyes to Jo's face. "Are you really?"

"Of course." Jo sat up straighter in her little chair. "Why would you think differently?"

"It's no secret you resented me, Jo. I know you felt like I tore up Walsh and Cam's friendship."

"You did." Not a muscle in Jo's face even twitched when she said it. Her face was as certain as her voice.

"Yeah, I did." Kerris settled back onto the stool, forcing herself to face Jo like she was facing her mistakes. "You don't have to condemn me. I feel guilty enough on my own."

"Cam was crazy about you, Kerris." Jo chewed a corner of her bottom lip. "Did you ever love him? Or was it always Walsh?"

"Those are two separate issues, Jo, believe it or not." Kerris pulled out the elastic holding her hair back from her face, dropping her head until the hair hid her expression before looking back up. "Yes, I did love Cam. And, yes, in some ways, it was always Walsh. I loved Cam, just not the way he deserved to be loved. Not as a wife should love her husband, and it was unfair of me to use him the way I did."

"Use him?" Jo pulled her fine brows together. "What do you mean?"

"It's a long story. Maybe once I've figured it all out myself, I'll tell you about it."

"And Walsh? Are you sorting things out with him, too?"

Kerris stared back at Walsh's cousin, unsure of how to answer.

"My divorce isn't even final. I'm not thinking of romance with anyone. And you?" Kerris hoped to divert the conversation away from the sordid little triangle that had been her relationship with Walsh and Cam. "Are you seeing anyone?"

"Me? No, I've been too busy. Aunt Kris left a huge hole in the foundation leadership, and I've had to step in and assume some of her responsibilities."

"That's wonderful, Jo. Kristeene would be so proud."

Jo nodded, glancing down at her lap before looking back up, her face less guarded than Kerris was used to seeing it.

"You know, this is all I've ever known. The foundation and what we do. I wasn't with a lot of kids my age growing up. By seven years old, I was already traveling with Aunt Kris." A small smile played around Jo's mouth, half pain, half humor. "One year we traveled the world together. She kept me out of school and tutored me herself. We went to Paris and Milan."

Jo looked down at her lap, stroking Kristeene's ring on her finger.

"We went to Uganda and Ethiopia. We held babies living in deplorable conditions in Chinese orphanages. Who cared about whatever I was missing with kids my age. I got a whole year of that. With her." Jo glanced up at Kerris, and it was like Kristeene was alive in her eyes. "That's who raised me. That's who raised Walsh. And in many ways, that's who raised Cam. She made us a family."

The words ambushed Kerris. She hadn't seen this coming and didn't want to go there with Jo, but insistence firmed itself on the other woman's face.

"They were all I had. My mother died before I knew her, but I had this incredible woman and this incredible unit. And for a while, I felt like you ruined that."

Kerris disciplined her mouth, refusing to let it tremble, denying the tears burning in her throat.

"The first time they met at camp, Walsh and Cam fought. Aunt Kris had to break it up. I never saw them fight again." Jo's silvery eyes dulled. "But the last time I saw them together, they were both bloody, fighting over you."

"They fought?"

"Yeah, they fought." Jo glanced around the room, at the festivity that continued even while they spoke. "I wanted to hate you, but I can't. Walsh loves you. Aunt Kris loved you."

Pain twitched Jo's face.

"Cam loves you."

That look when Jo said Cam's name was so completely different from anything else, Kerris couldn't help but study the other woman an extra moment or two. The lines of Jo's face, usually guarded and disciplined, softened. She bit her bottom lip and ran her palms along the silk of the skirt she wore. She closed her eyes briefly, and Kerris could see Jo clamp the emotion welling up to the surface.

"Jo, you love Cam, don't you?"

For a moment Kerris was sure Jo would deny it, but maybe her face was too tired to hide the truth anymore.

"Yeah, I love him." Jo stood up, the glance she ran over Kerris close to a dismissal. "And you didn't. You promised me on your wedding day that you'd take care of him. You told me you loved him. You lied to me."

In the face of the kind of selfless love Kerris read for Cam in Jo's eyes, there was no defense for how she had abused the other woman's trust. She could explain that she had never felt good enough for Walsh. Could say she had assumed he'd marry Sofie. Could even say Cam had known what he was getting into. But none of that would do any good. So she said the only thing that might.

"Jo, I'm sorry. Will you forgive me?"

Jo towered over Kerris with her height and her will. Just when Kerris thought Jo might haul off and slap her, her face conceded the kind of grin they hadn't shared in a long time.

"Get things fixed between my boys." Jo offered an uncharacteristic wink. "And I'll think about it."

Chapter Fourteen

When Mama Jess had turned Walsh away a year ago, Kerris believed the months would be covered in molasses. A slow drip. In some ways it had been just like that. The days she forced herself out of bed, forced herself to be with people, forced herself to smile—those were the days she measured in slow, painful breaths and the weight of loneliness. In other ways, the minutes, hours, and days had moved at the speed of sound, thrown ahead and waiting for her to catch up.

She and Cam had lived apart for a year, and according to North Carolina law, Cameron Raymond Mitchell and Kerris Moreton Mitchell could officially dissolve their marriage. Cam's lawyers, efficient rascals that they were, had already worked out all the details so the divorce could zip right through the system. The papers were here, already signed by Cam, awaiting her signature. They had agreed to walk out of the marriage with what they had come into it with. Cam had acquired a lot more than she had over the last few years, considering the money Kristeene had left him, but Kerris wanted none of it. It was so simple. So easy. So clean.

And yet, the typed words blurred under Kerris's teary eyes. She saw her failure, her selfishness, her faithless heart woven between the lines of text. That kiss with Walsh had been the domino that fell and started the downward spiral of her marriage. The beginning of the end. Or had the end begun when she said "I do," knowing she didn't, couldn't, love Cam the way he deserved to be loved?

She tightened her trembling fingers around the pen, blinking away the last of her tears and signing the papers. Half of her heart moaned because this was it, but the other half—those chambers she couldn't hide from any longer—whispered one name.

Walsh.

The thought of being with him made her ache and burn, twisted her heart around itself. Though the divorce wouldn't be official for another few months, she knew it was only a matter of time before he came to her. Would he even wait? She hoped so. She hoped not.

Kerris was still wrestling with the same riot of emotions when she entered her therapist Dr. Stein's office later that afternoon. Dr. Liza Stein was a gravedigger, exhuming the cadavers of past hurts, starting with Amalie and working her way backward. She had been unable to fully explore what Amalie had meant to Kerris without touching on Cam. And, of course, Dr. Stein had picked up the thread of that pain, Cam's departure, and followed it to her foster parents, and Mama Jess, and, finally, her mother.

It was hard for Kerris to accept that she had abandonment

issues, but it seemed that was the case. Would she even have married Cam at all if she'd had someone like Dr. Stein in her life earlier? Immediately after the rape, or when she was a teenager? Well-meaning counselors and teachers had recommended it before, but she'd never done the interior work this process demanded, and she'd probably regret it for the rest of her life.

You shouldn't cry over spilled milk, but there were so many innocent bystanders who had been splashed by her sloppy attempts to feel whole, to feel wanted and secure and like someone worth sticking around for. Namely, Cam and Walsh. Casualties of her insecurity and, dare she admit it, selfishness. She didn't just cry over the milk she had spilled. She mourned it, and wondered how she could ever make amends.

Dr. Stein didn't believe in a lot of preliminaries and pleasantries. She dove right in, and it wasn't long before she had Kerris confessing her guilt about the divorce, which was moving ahead with speedy inevitability.

"Kerris, do you want to stay married to Cam?"

"No, I definitely don't." Kerris shifted on the couch, glancing at the petite therapist with her stylish auburn bob and cat-eye glasses. "But he deserved someone else. He deserved better. I married him knowing I didn't love him the way I should."

"And did he know that? Did he walk into this with his eyes open?"

"Well, he knew I didn't love him that way." Kerris hesitated, not wanting to broach a subject she had managed to avoid. "He may have even suspected how I felt about Walsh."

"Walsh?" Dr. Stein pounced. "And who is that? Where does he figure into all this?"

Kerris laid out her history with Walsh and Cam, piece by piece, detail by detail. She searched Dr. Stein's face for condemnation, for censure, but saw only professional impassivity, and the occasional gleam of sympathy.

"Kerris, what holds your heart back from Walsh?"

Nothing. Absolutely nothing held her heart back from Walsh. What she felt for him was tidal. It had crashed past her sense of right, had swept over her vows. He had capsized her heart.

"Um...I'm not sure I understand the question."

"Do you love Walsh Bennett?"

Kerris closed her eyes. She couldn't say that aloud, not today, especially with the divorce papers just now beginning their three-month journey through the legal system.

"Well, I...I care deeply about him," Kerris edited, hoping Dr. Stein would, just this once, leave this one stone unturned.

No such hope.

"Kerris, this works only if you're honest with me and with yourself. You know that."

Dr. Stein laid her glasses aside, her eyes sharper without the lenses.

"You've already admitted you married Cam knowing you had feelings for his best friend. And you've done what adults do when they realize they've made mistakes. You've owned that. Healthy people can own their mistakes and, over time, move on. You've taken huge steps toward that, and I applaud you. Can you own this emotion? Do you love Walsh?"

Kerris looked down at the brightly patterned sundress she wore, tracing the paisley swirls with her finger, wishing she could disappear into the design, be consumed by the color and pattern.

"Kerris, I asked you a question."

Kerris shook her head, setting the silver bells in her earrings jingling.

"No, you don't love him, or no, you won't answer?" Dr. Stein leaned forward, those unrelenting eyes never leaving Kerris's face.

"I…I don't want to talk about this. Not today," Kerris said. "To say it while I'm still married to Cam, it just feels wrong."

"Kerris, don't judge your feelings. Don't avoid them. Own them. If you feel something, you have to voice it. Have you made any progress on the other thing we discussed last week?"

Kerris froze, unsure which poison she'd choose. Talking about Cam and Walsh or talking about…

"Amalie," Dr. Stein reminded her unnecessarily. "You were going to finally visit her grave."

Not a morning went by without Kerris thinking about her little girl, and some days the pain was as fresh as it had been when she woke up with an empty womb. Other days it was a dull ache, distracting, but not consuming. She'd think she was getting better, putting that behind her, only to burst into tears at the sight of a mother and child in the park, or at the grocery store.

"Have you given any more thought to that?" Dr. Stein asked.

"Um, I have."

"You have visited, or you have given more thought to it?"

"I thought about it some more, and I will do it soon." Kerris stood, glancing at her watch. "Looks like we're done."

"I say when we're done," Dr. Stein corrected, her voice like a hammer wrapped in fluffy cotton. "We have three minutes left. I'd like to spend these last three minutes talking about Amalie."

"I can't." Kerris gulped, blinking back the tears thoughts of her baby girl often brought to her eyes. "I'm not ready."

"You've made so much progress over the last year." Dr. Stein wrote something in the margins of her notes before standing to face Kerris. "Please don't think I'm not proud of you. I am, but there's a next level. And to get there, you're going to have to deal with both of these issues. Amalie, and your relationship with

Walsh. If you don't want to end up hurting him the way you hurt Cam, you need to be honest and figure out what you really want from him and for both of you."

Dr. Stein voiced Kerris's fear. That she would hurt Walsh. That as much as she cared for him, as much as he meant to her, as deeply as she felt connected to him, that her damaged self would hurt him. She couldn't live with that. And yet, the thought of him made her throb. Not just him physically, but his gentleness, his intuition, his sensitivity, his intensity, his strength. Could she really do the hard work it would take for all of that to be hers? Did she even deserve it?

* * *

A week later, Kerris was no closer to peace. She'd been wrestling with the issues Dr. Stein unearthed. The past was a labyrinth she couldn't find a way out of. With every turn she took, she hoped it would lead to an exit to a new life, a new chapter, but each turn just looped her back into old memories, old patterns, old hurts. Sometimes, alone outside, Kerris could work things out that made no sense when she was indoors, so she set out for her garden.

"Mama Jess, I'm out back picking greens and tomatoes."

Kerris let the screen door slam behind her, stomping toward the garden. She'd spent a lot of time out there in the week since she'd sent off the divorce papers. Seemed like this garden was a form of therapy all its own.

Kerris grabbed the bucket they always left at the garden gate, and slipped on her hot-pink Hunter rain boots. She rolled up the sleeves of the men's shirt she'd snatched up from the Salvation Army thrift store last week, the tail of the oversize shirt flowing to mid-thigh. With the shirt completely covering her tiny cutoff denim shorts, and the hot-pink rain boots covering her calves up to her knees, she didn't want to think about the picture she made. She looped her hair up into a knot on top of her head, secured with a wooden spoon.

She started down a row of tomatoes, bucket in hand, squatting to inspect the first bushel, not turning when she heard Mama Jess come up behind her.

"I think you were right about these tomatoes, Mama Jess." She tossed the words over her shoulder, moving onto the next bushel. "Still a lot of green. We do have a few in the house, though, right? I was gonna make a salad tonight for myself since you'll be off playing bingo."

Kerris stepped across a couple of rows, careful to avoid the still-growing vegetation. She reached down to caress a collard green leaf.

"These are ready, though," she said to the still-quiet Mama Jess. "I'll pull some of these and we can have them for dinner tomorrow night. How's that sound?"

The woman wasn't this quiet even when she was asleep.

"Did you hear—"

Kerris turned, and the words froze in her throat and then melted under the heat of Walsh's gaze. He was still on the tomato row, a few feet behind her, incongruous with his tailored slacks and his expensive shoes planted in the dirt of her garden.

"Walsh." She dropped her bucket.

"Kerris." The brewing storm in his eyes said the evenness of his tone was a lie.

"Why are you here?" One hand flew up to her messy hair and the other tugged the tail of her Salvation Army shirt.

"Somehow I thought that would be obvious." Walsh took the steps necessary to bring him to her row.

"I'm not— My divorce isn't final yet." She took a step back and over into a row of peas. "Cam and I have lived apart for a year, but we still have a few months before things are final."

Walsh followed her, stepping over a row of collard greens. He reached out to capture her hand. She tried to free herself, but he held firm.

"Stop running from me." His soft words were an entreaty, a command, and a caress all bundled up in one unavoidable knot.

"I'm not running." She knew it was a lie, but she couldn't help it. "I just don't think it's a good idea for you to be here…yet."

"And I'm tired of waiting," he whispered, taking another step forward, using his index finger to tilt up her chin. "Don't send me away again. I've missed you."

She nodded, closing her eyes in the sweetest torture. His mouth brushed hers lightly, once and then again.

"Don't do this," she said, his breath hot against her parted lips.

His traced his tongue across her bottom lip.

"Do what?"

"That."

She shook her head, helpless, sure that he was going to kiss her and certain that she would not be able to send him away.

Walsh dipped his head, hovering over her open mouth for a few seconds, and she breathed him in before he possessed her mouth completely. He nudged her lips open wider, dipping his tongue into her mouth. He groaned at the shy brush of her tongue against his. He slid his hands down to her waist, pulling her close until her body's soft curves melted into the harder lines of his own. Desire simmered between them, a slow burn that steadily licked away at their control until there was nothing left but an open flame.

Kerris leaned into him, her hands plowing their way up his

chest and around his neck. Lips, tongue, teeth, famished and feverish. She was lost in him, oblivious to the world, pulled into the vortex of a kiss deeper and hotter than any she'd had before. His large, warm hand slipped under her shirt, stroking the naked skin of her back. He left her mouth long enough to scatter kisses down her neck and into the open collar of her shirt, whispering across the bones.

"A year. You've made me wait a year."

"Walsh, we—"

"And I'd wait another year, if I had to." He firm lips curved against her mouth. "But don't make me."

"Thought I told you to take it slow," Mama Jess said from the screen door.

Kerris tried to pull back, but Walsh trapped her against him, looking over Kerris's shoulder at Mama Jess with both brows raised.

"I *have* been taking it slow," he said.

"Didn't look slow to me."

"Why are you watching?" He laughed, pulling Kerris to his side and heading back toward the cottage.

"I gotta keep an eye on you with my girl." Mama Jess frowned, but her lips twitched with a smile she wouldn't give in to.

"I'll take care of *my* girl." Walsh looked down at Kerris, his eyes going a little softer and hotter. "Don't you have a bingo game or something that would take you away from the house for a few hours?"

Mama Jess laughed outright, placing a hand on her hip and sticking a stern finger in Walsh's face.

"Just because I'm out of the house don't mean you gettin' in, if you know what I mean."

"All righty then." Kerris stepped away from Walsh's possessive grip, mortified. "Um, so bingo?"

"Yes, bingo." Mama Jess narrowed one eye up at Walsh. He looked right back. "But I'll be back."

"And I'll be here." Walsh slipped his fingers between Kerris's.

As soon as the door closed behind Mama Jess, Walsh pulled her close for another kiss.

"Hey." Kerris protested, holding up a hand to push against his chest. "Let's talk."

"Talking's low on my list right now."

"Walsh, you can't just walk in here unannounced and expect…"

"Expect what? That you missed me as much as I missed you?"

She moved behind the couch to put some distance between them. "You can't just—"

"Please stop telling me what I can't do." Walsh frowned across the space she'd imposed between them. "What's wrong? I thought you'd be happy to see me."

"Walsh, I'm not divorced."

"It's only a matter of time." He came around the couch to take both of her hands in his.

"Yes, time. Something I asked you to give me."

"Something I gave you. A year's worth. I'm done with it."

"Oh, so that's it, because you're done?" She shrugged her slim shoulders under the thin cotton of the shirt. "You say time's up, so forget what I want."

"You want me to go?" Walsh's knife-sharp words sliced into the silence she had no idea how to fill.

Kerris looked down at the floor, not sure what to say. Every cell in her body burned for him. Her hands still shook from that kiss, but she was paralyzed. Leave? Stay? She knew if he stayed, it would be the beginning of something she wouldn't be able to stop, maybe ever. And if he left…the throb of loneliness would return. Even surrounded by friends, living a full life, missing him was a constant ache.

She looked up to see him striding toward the door, leaving. She wanted to do what was right, and for once she couldn't figure it out. Was it right to begin a relationship with Walsh before her divorce from Cam was final? Would that make the road to reconciliation between the friends that much harder? Would it alienate Cam even more? Was there any hope either way? She didn't know. The only thing she did know was that Walsh had breathed life into something that had been dead inside of her since the last time she saw him, and she couldn't let him go.

"Walsh!" She ran across the cobblestones, reaching him as he opened the car door.

He turned toward her, his expression masking the emotions she knew were churning inside of him. The same emotions churning inside of her. He didn't speak. He waited.

"Stay."

He closed his eyes, and finally breathed, relief let loose on his face. He wrapped his arms around the small of her back.

"Stay." She had to say it again. She rose on her tiptoes and folded her arms around his neck. "I'm sorry. I'm just confused, and I want to get this right."

"It *is* right, baby." He pulled back, and where she knew her eyes must be troubled, his were completely clear. "*We* are right. You know that. Don't listen to any voice but mine. Okay?"

"Walsh, Cam—"

"I don't want to hear about Cam. Cam is our past."

"He's your best friend."

"The hell he is. He abandoned you. He…Look, the last thing I want to talk about is your ex-husband."

"He's not my ex-husband yet. That's what I'm trying to tell you."

"How many ways can I tell you that I don't care?"

"Maybe I do."

"Maybe you should feed me. I'm starving."

As if on cue, his stomach let out a loud growl. He laughed down at her, triumphant.

"See? I told you."

"How'd you do that?" She pulled away to look at his stomach with healthy respect and suspicion.

"It's a gift. One of many."

"Well, I hope leftovers will satisfy that growl."

"Lead the way." Walsh gestured for her to precede him back to the cottage.

An hour later, they sat at the kitchen table with a feast of leftovers spread out in front of them. They caught up on each other's lives, rediscovering the easy rhythm of conversation they'd always shared. He loved hearing about the things she still did with the foundation, and was interested in her therapy sessions with Dr. Stein. She was excited to hear how much time he'd spent with his father, and sympathized when he voiced regret that Bennett Enterprises was taking him away from his work with the foundation more and more.

"Mom would be disappointed in me." Walsh slid his finger up and down his glass of freshly squeezed lemonade, wiping away the condensation. Kerris didn't take him up on his casual tone. She knew the weight of that statement.

"I don't think she'd be disappointed." Kerris reached over to stop his finger and grab his hand. She waited for him to look at her. "You're still working with the foundation. Just less. She knew your focus would be with the business the older you got. It'll be yours one day. You have to prepare for that kind of responsibility."

Walsh squeezed her hand, showing her the truth of that in the eyes he usually guarded.

"I miss her."

"How could you not?"

"She was amazing." He used his other hand to shove a fork loaded with collard greens into his mouth. "And an amazing cook. I probably shouldn't say this, but I think Mama Jess's soul food is better than my mother's."

Kerris's smile started as such a little thing and then grew until it took over her face.

"This food?" She gestured with her own fork to encompass the dishes they had dug into and in some cases cleaned out.

"Bad, right?" Walsh smiled around a mouthful of greens. "I hadn't tasted food better than Mom's, but I gotta give credit where credit is due. Mama Jess's is even better."

Kerris couldn't stop smiling. She sliced apple pie for them both, standing and crossing to the freezer for vanilla ice cream. She plopped a scoop of ice cream onto his apple pie, laughing when he pulled her into his lap.

"Walsh Bennett!" She hooked one elbow around his neck. "I want my pie."

"Okay." He secured her in his lap with one arm and reached around to the table with the other. He forked up a hunk of the gooey dessert with ice cream, poising it before her mouth. She lunged forward to capture it, pretend pouting when he pulled the fork farther out of reach.

Walsh finally slid the fork into her mouth, his eyes locking with hers as she chewed, self-conscious under his stare.

He leaned in, pulling her chin down and her mouth open, chasing the hot and cold sweetness on her tongue. Kerris wasn't sure what was better, the pie or the taste of Walsh. She moaned, leaning closer into him, pressing her slight weight fully against him. He turned her, settling her thighs on either side of his, sliding his hands down the bare legs straddling him. He reached under her shirt to caress her back.

"Whose damn shirt is this?" he said against her mouth, licking at the corners and biting her bottom lip.

"Huh?" She clutched his shoulders, blinking through a passion-fogged daze.

"This is a man's shirt." He pulled back, placing both hands at her waist, steadying her on his lap. "Whose shirt is it?"

"What?"

"Kerris." He laid his palm against the side of her face and traced the sensitive skin behind her ear. A shiver skittered from the tender spot down her spine. "The shirt."

"Sorry." Focus. "It's just one I picked up at the Salvation Army."

"Oh." Walsh's expression cleared. He leaned in again, nibbling around her mouth.

"Why?"

It was Kerris's turn to pull back. She looked at him, putting her hand between her mouth and his. He kissed her sensitive palm, running his tongue between her fingers. The moist swipe of his tongue sent a jolt skidding across her hand. She forced herself to lean back another inch, her breasts heavy and aching to press against his solid chest.

"I thought…I wasn't sure if…" Walsh fixed his eyes over her shoulder. "I thought it might be one of Cam's."

She peered at him through her lashes, her blood slowing, losing the hot press through her veins.

"And that would have bothered you?"

"Yeah. Probably. I don't know."

Walsh kissed down her neck, pushing his hand into her hair, dislodging it. Her hair spilled around her shoulders and down her back. Walsh chinned aside her shirt collar, dipping his head to kiss the shallow indentation at the base of her neck. Kerris forced herself to scoot off Walsh's lap and turn to face him, almost laughing at the disoriented look on his face at finding his arms and lap suddenly empty.

"I'm married to Cam, Walsh. We can't ignore that."

Walsh sat back, propping one elbow on the back of the chair and sliding his long legs forward into a lazy pose that didn't fool Kerris.

"You're divorcing Cam."

"No, he's divorcing me."

"Whatever." He opened his arms. "Come back."

"No, let's talk about this. There's an elephant in the room."

"I thought I liked Dr. Stein." Walsh dropped his arms and leaned forward to rest his elbows on his knees. "But I think she may have you talking about your feelings a little too much. Ker, I don't want to talk about Cam, and I definitely don't want to fight about Cam. Not today."

"Walsh, the shirt. It obviously bothered you enough to ask."

"Kerris, the shirt is the least of what bothers me." Walsh stood up, taking a step closer. "Meredith would post pictures on Facebook during your pregnancy. I was blown away by how beautiful you were, and it tore me up that it was with someone else's baby. Do you get that?"

"Walsh, let's not—"

"No, you wanted to talk about our feelings. Well, I felt like hurling my computer across the room every time there was a post about an ultrasound, or names you were considering, or whatever. The baby wasn't *mine*, Kerris. And it gutted me."

Kerris wasn't sure what to say. She started gathering dirty

dishes from the table, scraping and rinsing them in silence before loading them into the dishwasher.

"I would have adored her, though," Walsh said so softly she almost missed it over the sound of running water.

"What?" She didn't turn to face him, her hands floating under the faucet.

"I would have adored Amalie." Walsh walked up behind her and took the plate from her numb fingers. He turned the water off. "I never wished she wasn't born. I just wished she was mine."

Kerris closed her eyes, but the tears slipped unchecked from under the tightness of her eyelids. Her shoulders shook with hurt and loss she hadn't realized she'd been saving up for this moment when she'd be with Walsh again. He turned her into his arms, the small of her back pressed against the sink.

"It's okay, baby," he whispered into her hair, stroking the silkiness of it.

"Still, Walsh. I'm still hurting over this." Kerris spilled her composure into a wet mess on Walsh's shoulder. Her temples throbbed with the force of the sobs shaking her body. "The last time I saw you I was blubbering all over you in the hospital room about her. And here I am, again…still broken up."

"It was a life, Kerris." Walsh pulled back, lifting her chin and forcing her to look in his face. "How long do you mourn a life that's lost? I mourn my mother all the time. Sometimes I find myself on the verge of tears in a stupid board meeting because it hits me that I'll never see her again. And I had almost thirty years with her. You had no time with Amalie, but she was a part of you. It'll get better, baby, but it probably won't ever go away completely."

Kerris buried her face deeper in the strength of Walsh's chest, tightening her arms around his waist. She breathed in the scent that was uniquely his, nothing to do with the expensive cologne he wore. She feathered kisses along his collarbone where the collar of his shirt fell away. His hands tightened around her waist, and he brought her so close she truly believed nothing would separate them again. He pulled her up on her tiptoes and left a sweet kiss behind her ear.

"Y'all were in the same position when I left," Mama Jess said from the kitchen door, frowning with her hands on her hips. "We need to talk about the definition of slow, Mr. Bennett."

Walsh looked at Mama Jess with his lips pressed together against laughter. Kerris, on the other hand, dropped her head to his shoulder, mortified...again.

"Walk me out." He reached down for Kerris's hand and pulled her past Mama Jess's disapproving figure. He dropped a quick kiss on Mama Jess's cheek. "Thank you for taking care of her for me."

"For *you*?" She huffed and puffed, but Kerris could see something melt in Mama Jess's eyes for Walsh, and wondered when he'd charmed himself into her good graces. "I don't think so."

Walsh only smiled and shrugged, heading for the front door and tugging Kerris behind him.

"Dinner was delicious, by the way," Walsh said to Mama Jess over his shoulder.

"Dinner? I didn't cook no dinner."

"We had the leftovers. Collard greens, rice and gravy, country fried steak. I told Kerris it was even better than my mom's."

"Kerris cooked that food last night for dinner." Mama Jess's grin held pride for her star pupil. "I taught her, though."

Walsh looked down at Kerris, running his finger along the curve of her jaw.

"Wow. Beautiful *and* an amazing cook. I hit the jackpot."

Kerris rolled her eyes to disguise her pleasure at his compliment, tugging on his hand and pulling him toward the front door. Between the embarrassment at being found playing kissy face, and the good ol' fashioned lust that kept catching fire in her belly every time Walsh looked at her, she was ready to make a quick exit.

"Why didn't you tell me that was your food?" Walsh chuckled, leaning against the car and pulling her between his legs once they were outside.

Kerris shrugged, shuffling her feet between his. She lowered her eyes to the ground, unable to see much in the dim light, but knowing if she looked at him much longer, she'd probably shove him against the car and have her way with him on the hood. Feeling like this, every moment infused with the heat flaring between them, how could she keep the pace she needed to heal? To do this right?

"My divorce will be final in three months. You could've waited those three months."

"Then send me away."

His face was a blank sheet of paper with all his emotions written in invisible ink. She could feel the tension creeping into his shoulders as he waited for her response.

"What?" She blinked. "I, um, I just think…"

"Say it. Say, 'Walsh, I don't want you here. Go away.'"

Kerris closed her eyes, relishing the smell of him. She could still taste him on her tongue. They were easy words to say. What if he actually left? After having him again for one night, she couldn't bear the thought of his absence, even for three months.

"Send me away." His whispered words got lost in the hair he had loosened against her neck. He ran his tongue along the fragile whorls of her ear, nipping her earlobe. He licked the shallow indentation behind her ear, smiling when she couldn't suppress a delighted shudder. "No?"

Kerris shook her head dazedly, leaning into him, plaiting her fingers with his. Her heart was a rocket in her chest, poised for takeoff. Fired and ready. She licked at the lips left dry by her passion-shallowed breaths. She looked up at him with helpless accusation, feeling like all her emotions were tangled up in him. He was wrapped around her, and she didn't want to get away.

"I'll see you tomorrow."

A smug smile played across his lips. His big hands came up on either side of her face. He kissed her, sipping from her like a well of fresh water. Holding her like she was glass in his hands, delicate and fragile, and he was afraid his love would break her.

"When tomorrow?" Walsh asked.

"I don't know. I'm working at Déjà Vu all day. After work?"

"What time is that?"

"It's ten to six." She leaned into his palm cupping the side of her face.

"I'll pick you up at six." The strong planes of his face were barely revealed in the moonlight, but she could see the tinder in his eyes. Felt the match strike of desire catch and pop inside with an answering fire. "Pack a bag."

Kerris's heart went locomotive, pumping, puffing, and coming off the rails.

"Walsh, we can't... We need to set some ground rules. I already feel guilty enough about how things happened."

"Ground rules. Okay." Walsh teased her lips with his breath. "We can kiss, right?"

Kerris's brain fogged a little with the promise of his lips, but she nodded her head in jerks.

"And I can touch you here?" He skimmed a finger over her nipple through the cotton shirt.

Kerris stepped back, afraid if this went much further they'd end up dry humping against a tree.

"Everything but." The words shot out of her mouth sharply, before she could round their edges.

Walsh rolled his eyes, but his smile stayed in place.

"I can do everything but, for now. I mean, you tortured me for the last year. I think I can last another three months."

Kerris looked up at him, tiny firecrackers going off everywhere his hands had touched.

"And you're fine with us not…well, with how I want to handle things. The fact that we can't—"

"We won't." He leaned down, pressing his lips behind her ear and down her neck, leaving a wake of sparks. "God knows I want to, though."

He pulled her closer, and feeling him hard and stiff against her softened the cartilage around her knees. She slumped a little and his fingers tightened on her elbows. She looked up and his green eyes, dark and hot and tender, were waiting for her.

"So tomorrow night, we are on our own. I love Mama Jess, Kerris, but I don't need a chaperone."

Kerris allowed her mouth a small grin.

"I just want us to have something we've never had," Walsh said. "Time uninterrupted. Alone."

"I know, Walsh, I just…"

"You trust me, Kerris?"

She always had. Almost from the beginning. Irrationally. Stupidly. Completely. With her secrets and, even though it wasn't his to take, with her heart.

"Yes."

"Good." He bent to leave the words on her lips. "Then pack a bag."

Chapter Fifteen

The tinkling bell above Déjà Vu's door signaled someone had entered the shop. Kerris trapped a sigh behind her lips. She recited all the reasons she should be pleasant and patient with this final customer. She owned this place. She was responsible for its success. Over the last year, while Kerris healed, inside and out, Meredith and Mama Jess had borne more than their share of the work here. Kerris didn't begrudge them this day off. So even though seeing Walsh tonight had dominated her thoughts all day, she needed to suck it up and be nice.

She closed the register drawer and looked up, the warmed-over smile freezing on her face when she saw her last "customer."

"Trisha?"

Kerris had barely gotten the name out before Walsh's assistant came behind the counter and pulled her into a perfume-scented hug.

"Kerris, you look awesome." Trisha's chocolaty eyes inspected Kerris from her Betty Boop T-shirt, her flared denim skirt, and up to the messy bun Kerris had pulled her hair into over the course of the day. "I mean, we have work to do, but I haven't seen you since the accident and you're in one piece, so you look awesome."

"Trisha, thank you? I think? And what work? What are you doing here?"

"Walsh sent me."

"From New York?"

"I flew in with him yesterday, yeah." Trisha looked around the shop. "You done here? We need to get going."

"Trisha, I hate to be slow, but what are you talking about? I thought Walsh was picking me up."

"Not exactly." Trisha ran a hand over her closely cropped burnished cap of hair. "We're meeting him."

"Okaaaaay." Kerris gave the shop one last glance and rushed over to flip the sign on the door to CLOSED before anyone else showed up. "Just let me get my things together."

Kerris grabbed her purse and the overnight bag she had promised Walsh she'd bring. Her fingers trembled around the handle. She couldn't sleep with Walsh, not while she was married to Cam. As deeply as her feelings ran for him, Ms. Kris was right. She had compared Kerris to the river whose course, once set, couldn't change. Kerris sometimes wasn't sure what was right, but when she knew, she wouldn't be swayed. And having sex with Cam's best friend when their divorce wasn't final? That wasn't right. That could not happen.

"Okay, I'm ready."

Kerris stepped back into the shop. Trisha was taking pictures with her phone of one of their display cases. She looked up, a grin creasing her golden brown cheeks.

"I forgot all about your jewelry." Trisha took one more shot of the Riverstone Collection Kerris had started selling in the shop a few weeks ago. "I'm sending these pics to my friend in New York I told you about."

"Really?" Kerris bit into the smile pulling at her lips. "Wow. Thanks."

"I'd forgotten how unique your stuff is. She'll flip." Trisha slipped her phone into the leather clutch on the glass display case. "Now we really need to go."

On the ride to wherever they were going, Trisha asked Kerris about her recovery from the accident and shed light on her part in getting Walsh to the hospital that night.

"I'm glad Meredith called me." Trisha flicked her eyes away from the road to glance at Kerris in the passenger seat. "I've always known Walsh felt something for you."

Kerris's cheeks heated up but she refused to retreat; to run away from these feelings, from her past mistakes, from this conversation. Dr. Stein would be so proud.

"How did you know?"

"I caught him looking at your picture on his phone a few times. Plus, you were on a very short list of people Walsh always wanted to have access to him no matter what." Trisha fixed her eyes on the road ahead. "So was Cam, of course. And I've seen how not having you both in his life has affected Walsh."

The Mercedes purred along, adding no sound to the uncomfortable silence filling the car.

"Trisha, Cam and I—"

"I'm not judging you, Kerris. You're separated, and if you ask me, based on what I've seen, this is how it should have always been." Trisha pulled into a parking space and put the car in park. "Come on. We're here."

"Here" turned out to be an isolated section of riverbank, deserted except for a lone houseboat floating near the water's edge.

"What's going on?"

"I like you, Kerris, but you're not worth losing my job." Trisha zipped her mouth. "My lips are sealed. Come on. We have work to do."

"What kind of work?"

Over the next hour, Kerris found out that beauty was indeed work. The houseboat might look unassuming from the outside, but it was tricked out with every modern convenience, including hardwood floors, gorgeous paneling, and a large bedroom suite.

One bedroom suite.

As soon as she entered the room, her breath caught. Not from how luxuriously decorated the room was, but from the dress spread on the bed. It was so simple and perfect. Some mixture of blush and nude, the A-line minidress would not overwhelm her petite frame. Kerris picked it up and checked the tag. Stella McCartney and her size. She grinned and held the dress against her chest.

"You got my size right."

"I didn't. Walsh did."

Kerris nearly dropped the dress, though her jaw did drop.

"Walsh chose this for me?"

"Yes. He has planned everything down to the last detail, so don't thank the messenger." Trish reached for the phone that was ringing in her purse. "Yes, we're already onboard. Hurry. We've got plenty to do in just a little time."

Kerris was admiring the nude heels on the floor in front of the bed when two girls walked in, loaded down with cases of products—makeup, conditioner, shampoo, wax, hair dryers, and flat irons. Trisha showed them through to the marble-tiled bathroom just off the bedroom.

"Most of your work will be done in here." Trisha gave both girls a smile and extended her hand, palm up. "As we discussed, I'll take your phones now. You'll get them back once you're done."

Kerris gave Trisha a puzzled look.

"Can't be too careful." Trisha slipped both phones into the pockets of her linen slacks. "The tabloids are always looking for any little morsel about Walsh's private life. You can understand why this...situation requires discretion."

Because Walsh lived a life people wanted to know about. In Hong Kong one day and back in his four-million-dollar New York apartment the next. Kerris wondered for a moment at her own audacity to think she could do this. That she might be able to occupy this world with him. Her? No money? No parents? A past littered with dirty details she never wanted anyone digging into. Just as she was about to flee the houseboat and hitchhike home if she had to, Dr. Stein's guidance reminded her of all the mistakes this kind of thinking had led her to make the first time.

That nagging voice in her head telling her she wasn't good enough? Telling her TJ had ruined her for someone like Walsh? Telling her she should settle for something less because she was damaged goods?

That voice lied.

And the truth was in the mirror two hours later, shining from her eyes. The truth was she loved Walsh. That girl staring back at her with the freshly washed shiny curls and the high-end dress and the new manicure and everything waxed and plucked and ex-foliated? She was the case, but the jewel was inside of her. The man she loved, loved her back. Thought of her as a miracle. And would go out of his way to make their first date this special.

"Thank you, ladies," Trisha said to the beauty battalion, as Kerris had come to think of them. "Great work. You'll get your phones once you're back on dry land."

"So what's next?" Kerris hoped it involved Walsh, because as much as she had enjoyed the beauty regimen and the pretty clothes, he was what she wanted.

"I'm leaving and Walsh will take it from here." Trisha gave the room one last glance, all business, but her eyes went personal when they landed on Kerris. "You look beautiful."

"Thanks." Kerris ran her eyes down the dress and heels, then touched the hair spilling over her shoulders and down her back. She looked back to Trisha, whose hand was already on the doorknob. "Thanks for everything."

"Enjoy tonight. Come on out when you're ready."

Kerris stood in the middle of the room for a few moments, absorbing all that had happened so far.

"Come out and go where?" Kerris asked the empty room.

She opened the door, and her attention was immediately drawn to a crystal-encrusted card on the floor in the dimly lit hallway, the first in a trail of cards telling her exactly where to go. The first card said FOLLOW. Kerris saw a trail of glittering cards until the message FOLLOW YOUR HEART TO ME led her up a shallow flight of steps and out onto the upper deck.

"Looking for me?"

Kerris turned in the direction of the voice she could pick out from a million others. Walsh stood by a small round table positioned near the boat rail. Tall, with his dark hair ruffled by the slight breeze rolling in with the setting sun, flawlessly tailored jacket molded to his broad shoulders, linen shirt left open at his tanned throat, hands in his pockets. A casual stance, but there was nothing casual about his eyes. They were ravenous, eating up every detail the beauty battalion had so painstakingly attended to.

He extended a hand to her.

"Come here, Kerris."

The words were spoken so softly she barely heard them over the water lapping up against the houseboat, but they commanded her. Those three words reached into her chest and pulled her to him by the heart. She was in his grip. Surely he knew that, but something in his eyes seemed to wonder if she would come.

With every step she took toward him, a certainty, just a seed before, went deep and rooted itself inside of her. She was his and he was hers. He had known it before she did. He had tried to tell her, but her fear, her self-doubt, her own insecurities, had sabotaged their first chance at happiness. Every step she took toward him was redemption, a declaration. A promise. Maybe she did still have some issues to work through about her mother, about TJ, about Amalie, about how she had mishandled things with Cam. The residue of those things might always coat her perspective, even if just a little. But Walsh was her bright future, and for once, she would grab what she truly wanted with both hands.

She didn't stop when she was close. She walked right past the hand he held extended and into his arms. She slid her hands up his shoulders, standing on her toes until she could hook her elbows behind his neck. He wrapped his arms around her, suspending her, and her toes left the ground. She pulled back just far enough to whisper in his ear.

"I'm sorry it took me so long."

Chapter Sixteen

The words she'd spoken burned his ears and flipped his heart. Walsh made a conscious effort to loosen his arms, which were auto-clamped around Kerris like she might disappear if he blinked. And it still felt that way. After so long, she felt like smoke in his arms. Like she'd dissipate if he didn't clutch her close enough. She pulled back and settled on her feet. In the heels he'd chosen especially for her, she was a few inches taller than she usually stood, but still barely made it to his shoulder. He'd always dated models and tall girls like Sofie. That this petite woman who stood heart-level in her bare feet had owned him so completely, effortlessly, almost from the beginning still amazed him.

"I know it's been a long time, but—"

"Worth the wait." He had to cut her off, dragging his thumb over one high cheekbone. "Don't ever doubt that you were worth the wait, Kerris."

The last few years had sliced him open, jerked out his insides, and stuffed everything back in messily, sloppily, haphazardly. Nothing had felt right until now. They still had a landmine to negotiate. Walsh had never dated anyone quietly. What had started as the media's casual interest in his love life even when he was in high school had only intensified when he dated Sofie, and hadn't dropped off nearly as much has he'd like. The three-ring circus of him dating his best friend's not-even-ex-yet-wife? Inevitable. Kerris would hate that. Walsh would hate it, too. This perfection between them—this connection of heart, mind, and soul—shouldn't be sensationalized. So he'd be discreet, but he had no intention of being subtle. Not tonight.

"Hungry?" He gestured to the table, already set with stuffed lobster tail, asparagus, and new baby potatoes.

Once she noticed the food, her eyes widened and she licked her lips. Walsh would wait his turn, but he planned to lick her lips, too. He pulled out her chair, leaning down to draw in the smell hidden behind her ears and along her neck. He'd made sure Kerris's vanilla scent was on Trisha's shopping list.

As easily as they had always talked with each other, there was little conversation over dinner. Walsh barely ate, doing no justice to the delicious meal he'd had delivered from Stream, the seafood restaurant in town. Kerris would glance up from her food and find him staring. She didn't bother to ask what he was looking at or if anything was wrong. Absolutely nothing was wrong. Things were finally right, and he almost couldn't believe it. Time for phase two. He glanced at his watch and reached across the table to take her hand.

"Do you remember that Fourth of July by the river?"

Kerris nodded, lowering her eyes to their clasped hands but not speaking.

"I was fighting so hard against wanting you." Walsh swallowed, taking a sip of his white wine before continuing. "Cam touched your hair and your face and I wanted to strangle him. You were his, but you felt like mine. Even then, you felt like mine."

"We laughed by the river." She smiled a little. "I still have the rock I found that day with you. The one you asked me about."

"I know we can't undo the past. The pain and the misunderstandings. How we hurt Cam." Walsh watched the moonlight caressing the river before looking back at Kerris, seeing the regret and hope warring in her eyes. "But there was one thing we didn't get to share together that day, and I thought maybe tonight we could."

"What was that?"

"Fireworks."

And right on time, based on Walsh's calculations, the sky flared and popped, light and fire exploding over the river. The fireworks display wasn't the show, though. The expression on Kerris's face made him her captive audience of one. She sped over to grip the rail. She covered her mouth to catch the laugh that sprang free, and Walsh could see she wasn't fully processing that he had actually arranged a fireworks display just for her. He watched it dawn on her, the laughter melting away and something very close to awe settling on her face.

He approached her at the rail. Their eyes locked and held, that same electric current passing between them that had fried his brain the first night he'd met her. That had branded his soul with her and only her ever since. He reached into his jacket pocket and withdrew a delicate chain. He turned her to face the fireworks while he laid the necklace against her heart and hooked the clasp behind her neck. She fingered the orchid charm suspended from the chain, an orchid made of Swarovski crystals, faceted and spectral against the creamy gold of her skin. The first time he had seen her, she'd worn an orchid in her hair. He would never see the flower again without thinking of her.

He didn't give her the chance to turn around, but clasped his arms around her waist, pulling her back against his chest. She looked up, tilting her head to see him standing behind her.

"It's beautiful." She stroked the orchid charm with one hand and pointed to the sky, still electrified with color, light, and sound. "It's all so beautiful. You'll spoil me."

Walsh moved his hands to her hips, turning her around to face him.

"Exactly my plan." He dusted kisses down the fragile line of her jaw and neck, inhaling the addictive scent that was only partly vanilla and mostly Kerris.

"Why, Walsh?" she whispered, her voice wavering and her eyes rimmed with tears. "Why me?"

"My heart didn't give me a choice. I saw you and was gone almost from the beginning." He was so close he could smell nothing but her, could see nothing but her, felt the warm curve of her waist beneath his hands. "You are the best decision my heart ever made."

Walsh didn't bend, but waited for her to come to him, and she did. On her toes again, she tunneled her fingers into his hair and gave him that beautiful lush mouth he'd possessed in his dreams more times than he could count. This wasn't a dream, though. And it wasn't frantic or rushed. She browsed his mouth, running her tongue along his teeth and licking into corners and crevices like they had all the time in the world. And maybe now they did.

"You trust me, right?" He whispered against her lips between kisses.

She nodded, squeaking when he lifted her and set her on the rail.

"I got you," he said, gripping her waist and pushing her thighs open so he could stand between them. "You in this dress, baby? Driving me crazy. I keep seeing these beautiful legs wrapped around my waist."

Kerris nodded, setting her elbows on his shoulders and caressing the back of his neck, bringing him back in for a kiss. Sucking his lips. Licking into his mouth. Nibbling at the corners. She never broke the kiss, but hooked her ankles behind his back, her slim legs tightening around his waist when he lifted her and stepped away from the rail. When he slid his hands to cup her butt and carried her down the shallow stairs to the one bedroom on the houseboat.

She flowed like water down his body when she loosened her legs and settled back on the floor. Walsh's fingers shook a little over the hidden zipper at the back of the short dress, the hiss of its teeth revealing her to him like a secret. This moment, the promise of this revelation, had tortured him ever since he'd seen the dress in the store. For their first date, he'd wanted her wrapped from head to toe in everything he had chosen. Taking possession of what was his in the only ways he could until her divorce was final.

"Walsh, remember we can't," she said in between kisses, her breath hot and sweet on his lips.

"I know. Everything but. I just want to see you."

He pulled back to hold her eyes, sliding the zipper all the way down and peeling the material over her shoulders and down her sleek arms, rolling it past the subtle dip of her waist and hips, past the rounded cheeks of her ass and down the tanned length of her legs.

Worth every penny. The Carine Gilson lingerie looked like it had been painted onto her body. He'd chosen the nude-colored sheer bra knowing that tonight he'd see her nipples pressing against the transparent fabric like ripe berries. Chosen the thong knowing he'd run his palms along the smooth, naked curves left completely exposed. Envisioned the dress pooling at her feet. What he hadn't imagined was the sweet color flushing her cheeks, or the way she looked at the floor and pulled her dark hair forward to cover her breasts. The way her breath stuttered in her chest or how she bit the corner of her mouth while she waited for him to say something.

He pushed the hair back over her shoulders and slid one hand behind her head, caressing with his thumb the soft hairs curling at her neck.

"No dream, no fantasy of you standing like this here in front of me could have prepared me for how beautiful you are, Kerris. You steal my breath."

He pulled her small hands to his chest, the truth of his words banging a frantic rhythm beneath his shirt because of her. It always had. He would spend the rest of his life making sure she believed him.

He would never ask her about the intimacy she had shared with Cam. It would be too much for him, and would ruin any chance, if there was still one, of them repairing their friendship. On one hand, he wasn't sure he even wanted Cam's friendship anymore. On the other, he wasn't sure that he deserved it. He knew how TJ had hurt Kerris and he knew Cam was the only man she had ever been with. Walsh knew that he himself would be her last lover. That was all that mattered anymore.

He dipped his head and licked the bow of her top lip, diving into her mouth, bobbing for her tongue. Tangling their lips and tongues in an intercourse between their mouths that left him heated and hard. Measuring their steps in inches, he guided her toward the bed he'd chosen for this room. For this night. When her knees hit the edge, he lowered her to the bed, stepping back to stare at the length of her body, blemished only by the few scars remaining from her accident, but still perfect to him. Would he be able to do this? Touch her? Taste her without taking her fully? Without finally coming home inside of her? He had lived without any of her for so long, but he could and he would control himself.

And he would enjoy every minute of it.

He knelt at the edge of the bed, and she came up on her elbows to watch him. He removed her shoes, taking one small foot in his hand. He kissed the high arch, licking at the fragile bone of her ankle. He ran his nose along the length of her calf until he reached her knee. He snared her eyes as he sucked behind her knee, grinning when her eyelids dropped and her elbows collapsed under her until she lay flat against the bed's silk duvet. He repeated the same ministrations with the other foot, loving her ankle, calf, and knee. He breathed kisses over her inner thighs until he reached her center, concealed by only a small triangle of silk.

He had to have some of her. He mouthed the hot, wet flesh through her panties, moaning at the taste of her exploding on his tongue. She arched off the bed, gripping his head and rolling her hips into the searching hunger of his mouth. He slid his hand up the silky skin of her waist until he reached her bra, pulling the fragile cup down and dusting his fingers across her nipple, so hard and tight. He lost himself in devouring her, loving her until she went completely still for a few moments, like she was absorbing every sensation. Then she cried out, splitting the quiet of the room down the middle with a dry sob that shook her shoulders and hoarsened her voice. Walsh pressed his face into the tremor of her thighs on either side of him, relishing the shake and shudder of her body surrendering to the first orgasm he had ever given her.

But certainly not the last.

Chapter Seventeen

Kerris woke up with Walsh's name on her lips. As vigilant as she had always been, careful in what she said and did, her dreams showed no such caution. Her dreams had always been wild horses. Charging past her inhibitions and morals, giving in to the desires she'd always checked when awake.

"I love that you say my name in your sleep."

Kerris panicked for a moment. Walsh was in her bed! She was used to waking up with his name on her lips and a guilty ache in her heart. Bed empty. Hope sagging. Frustrated and a little horny. Instead she felt sated, limbs weighted with leftover pleasure. Her sleep-fuzzed brain cleared second by second until last night snapped into focus. She had come more than once. And so had he, but they hadn't crossed that line. It was a technicality, one most people wouldn't care about, but one she clung to. One she needed.

She pushed back against the warm wall of muscle at her back. Walsh's hands wandered, lifting the gown he'd given her to wear last night, running his hands along her stomach and between her breasts until he reached the orchid charm she'd worn to bed. She turned over, and it was surreal to see Walsh's broad shoulders, the muscles stacked in his stomach, his dark green eyes and bed-rumpled hair, first thing in the morning.

"Did I say your name?" Kerris pulled her brows together and pushed her lips to one side. "Are you sure?"

"Oh, I'm sure that after last night I recognize my name on your lips."

Kerris's mouth rounded into an "o" and she buried her face in his shoulder.

"Walsh, good grief."

"Are you embarrassed?" He chuckled, nudging her shoulders until she was pressed back against the Egyptian cotton sheets and he was propped on his elbows, hovering over her. "I think I said your name a time or two myself."

"I just…this situation will take some getting used to. That's all."

"Am I a situation?" He breathed the words against her neck, tracking his lips up to draw her earlobe between his lips, between his teeth.

Embarrassment withered and died as desire, hot and urgent, came alive. Kerris turned her head, intercepting his mouth, moaning into the kiss as his hands pushed the silk gown up over her hips. A strident ringing stilled them both, lips pressed together, Walsh hard between her thighs. He dropped his forehead to hers, huffing a frustrated breath.

"That's my dad's ring tone."

Kerris tapped his shoulder for him to move.

"Get it! I will not be responsible for—"

He covered her open mouth with his, gripping her hip and grinding into her, taking her breath and every thought hostage.

"It's totally your fault," he whispered against her lips. He rolled over to sit on the side of the bed and grabbed his phone from the bedside table. "Hey, Dad."

Kerris eyed the tanned, muscled terrain of Walsh's back, tapering to his hips and butt. If she had thought of herself as a frozen river at one time, she was anything but now. She was a hot spring, rising and steaming and gushing every time she was around this man.

"Dammit, don't tell me that." Walsh leaned one elbow on his knee and ran his fingers through the dark hair curling around his neck.

Kerris rolled out of bed, letting the ivory and black silk of her gown float down her legs. She had never worn anything like it. And the matching kimono? Kerris smiled and tied the sash at her waist. Draped in decadence. That's how she felt. The real decadence? The hours they'd spent making that bed an altar where they worshipped each other's bodies. The true luxury? A night in Walsh's arms, falling asleep to reckless dreams and waking up safe in his love.

And now it was time for food.

She hadn't seen a kitchen last night, but this place seemed to have everything else. She assumed there was a place to cook and food to eat. She stepped toward the door, only to have Walsh snag her wrist and pull her to stand in front of him.

"Yep, I hear you, Dad." Walsh dropped kisses on her silk-covered stomach, caressing the curve of her butt. "I'll keep that in mind."

Kerris ran a hand over the unruly dark hair she had tugged last night as he pleased her unbearably. He looked up, his eyes soft, his grin a beautiful slash across the plane of his face. He patted her backside and turned her toward the door.

"Yeah, I'm still here," he said into the phone.

Kerris opened the bedroom door for the first time since last night when Walsh had brought her to bed wrapped around him like a lusty, clingy vine. Up on deck, the sun shone so brightly she squinted and sheltered her eyes with her hand. She explored the houseboat for a few minutes before she found the kitchen. Sure enough, it was fully stocked with everything she needed for pancakes and eggs.

Kerris was preparing an omelet when Walsh walked in wearing only boxers. Her mouth watered but not for the food. He stepped behind her, pulling her into his chest. Kerris leaned back into him, simultaneously comforted and excited by the hard strength of him encompassing her.

"I have to go back to Saudi."

Kerris turned the stove off and slumped her shoulders an inch.

"When do you leave?"

"In the morning."

"Oh. I just thought we'd have more time."

"I planned for us to have a week together." Walsh pulled her hair into one fist and smoothed the length of it. "I didn't count on a stubborn sheikh needing me to hold his hand until this deal is signed."

Kerris loaded food onto their plates and moved away to set them on the table. She blinked back foolish tears. She was the one who had sent him away for a year. And here she stood, puddling on the floor because he was leaving.

"I understand." She put forks down and poured orange juice, not looking at him in case he saw how disappointed she was.

"Baby, if I could get out of this I would." Walsh sat down to eat. "Dad's flying through to pick me up in the morning, and we're flying straight there."

Kerris was once again reminded how vastly different his life was from hers. She'd never even been out of the country, and Walsh hopped private jets like they were city buses. All her doubts that she could live in his world and share his life flooded her mind.

"Maybe it's a blessing in disguise." Kerris looked up, fiddling with the charm at her neck. "Things are moving fast. A little space might be good."

"Space?" Walsh wrapped an arm around her waist and slid her chair as close to his as possible. "We had a year of that. The last thing we need between us is space. Why don't you come with me?"

"Oh, yeah. I can see the headline now. 'Small-Town Girl Torn Between Two Lovers.' The press would have a field day."

"Baby, I'm not going to hide us."

"Walsh, I'm not asking you to hide." Kerris pulled back an inch to look at him. "I just want to be discreet."

"Discretion is a habit for me, Kerris. I've been living with media attention for a long time." He lifted her chin, his eyes resolved. "But I won't pretend we're not together, and anyone who sees us in the same room will know I'm completely whipped."

"You're not—"

"I am." He left the words on her lips. "I so am."

Kerris closed her eyes, unable to hold back from him when he was giving her so much.

"I don't want you to go." Kerris dropped her forehead to his chest before looking up. "I'm tired of missing you."

"Come with me." His earnest eyes trapped hers. "I want you with me."

"I can't just leave Mama Jess and Meredith with all the responsibility." Kerris gave a definitive shake of her head. "They've done so much while I recovered. It wouldn't be fair."

"But if we—"

"Please don't tempt me." She supplicated with just a glance. "I want to pull my weight at the shop, and it would be irresponsible just to drop everything and go. This is hard enough."

Walsh's head dropped back until he was looking at the ceiling. He brought his eyes back level with hers.

"Okay, I won't make it any harder. But don't expect to leave this houseboat today. We still have a lot of catching up to do." He pulled her into his lap. "Do you have any idea how many times I've imagined you like you were last night? Not just your body. You across a dinner table from me. Us in bed laughing and talking. It was perfect."

Kerris walked her fingers up his chest and around his neck. She met him halfway for a knee-weakening kiss.

"Everything far exceeded my imagination, Walsh."

"Oh, so you've imagined me?"

His eyes teased her, but the memory of having only her imagination sobered her. Daydreaming in the tub. Drifting off while cooking dinner to meet Walsh in her mind. Only having him in her dreams, and feeling guilty every time.

"As much as I dared, yes."

Walsh's eyes lost the laugh, but held on to the tenderness.

"I'm right here now. Save your dreams for our future. I wanted our first night together to be...what it was."

"Some first date. The fireworks. This beautiful necklace. The dress. The kimono. Are you trying to buy my affections, Mr. Bennett?"

"Pretty sure I already have your affections."

Kerris hit his bare chest.

"Arrogant!"

"Pretty sure you already knew that."

"You're right. I did. So do you treat all your first dates that way?"

He dropped his lashes, shielding his eyes before looking back at her, eyes serious and probing.

"Only my last first date."

Her divorce wasn't final. They'd just had their first date last night. She cleared her throat. What was she supposed to say to that?

"Um...your food's getting cold. Aren't you hungry?"

He laid his lips against hers.

"I'll let you get away with it for now. And yes, after waiting all this time to be with you? Starved."

"Food, Walsh." She smiled into their kiss. "I meant for food."

It felt so normal, so good, so right to be with him first thing in the morning. Doing things normal people did. They had always experienced each other only in stolen snatches, creating a mystique that compounded the intensity of their connection. Kerris had wondered how it would withstand the mundane. It was holding up rather nicely.

"This is nice, right?" Walsh asked, echoing her thoughts.

Kerris nodded and smiled around a mouthful of pancake.

"You look so happy. How can I arrange to spend every morning like this for the rest of my life?"

Kerris sobered, laying her fork down and moving to get up from his lap. His comment could lead them down a dangerous path. Walsh trapped her against him.

"Okay. I'm sorry. I'll drop it. Just stay right here. I hate it when you run from me."

"I'm not running." The lie soured the sweetness of syrup in her mouth. There were many things she was still running from. "I'm right here."

"I mean running in here." Walsh laid his hand against her heart.

He must have felt that stupid, traitorous muscle pounding furiously through the thin silk of her gown and kimono. His hand brushed against the soft curve of her breast, and she pressed herself deeper into his roughened palm.

He pushed the kimono away from her shoulders, allowing the silken folds to gather and hang at her elbows. Slowly, looking into the storm of desire she knew was gathering force in her eyes, he pushed the straps down her arms and watched the gown puddle around her waist. He swallowed hard at the sight of her naked breasts, rounded and full. He dipped his finger into the syrup on his plate, hovering over one nipple. Her chest heaved with the wait, every cell in her body impatient for his touch. The wicked passion lighting his eyes only intensified the torturous seconds before he slowly massaged the sticky syrup onto one nipple.

His fingers rubbed the syrup into the sensitive flesh, making Kerris gasp. Her eyelids dropped, white flags signaling her complete surrender. And then he was at her breast, the hot, wet worship of his tongue suckling the syrup away, laving the puckered areola.

"Ah."

That one syllable was all Kerris could spare. He had stolen her next breath, stolen her next thought. She pressed into the heat of his hungry mouth, clutching his head to her breast. Her head fell back, and the rhythmic suckling of his lips and tongue was so beautifully erotic she wanted to shove the dishes to the floor, drag Walsh up to the table, and slather syrup over every inch of his body. There were acres of hardened flesh to explore and worship in kind.

Kerris pulled him away from her breast and their lips collided, their tongues tangling, until she heard only one thing. The beating of her heart.

Chapter Eighteen

Y ou ever heard you can't make a pot of water boil faster by looking at it?" Meredith's eyes never left the spreadsheet she was studying on her laptop. "Same thing applies to that phone. Checking it every two minutes won't make it ring."

Kerris slid the phone into the pocket of her cotton dress and rearranged a few pieces from her Riverstone Collection on a shelf against the wall.

"What time was he supposed to call?" Meredith closed her laptop and stretched the muscles Kerris knew must be fatigued. Her friend had been at it all day.

"Five o'clock." Kerris ruined her pout with a smile. "But I'm sure there's a good excuse. His dad's a real slave driver. It's been hard for him to come here every weekend this month."

"But you're glad he has." Meredith slid her glasses up into her spiky, cotton candy–pink hair.

Kerris answered with only a smile, her hand straying toward the phone in her pocket again, but she caught herself in time. Walsh would call soon. He always called.

On the few occasions they had "gone public" since Walsh had returned from Saudi Arabia three weeks ago, he'd been approached by everyone from the mayor to the neighborhood busybodies, all of them shooting speculative glances between Cam Mitchell's best friend and his soon-to-be-but-not-yet-ex-wife. And each time she cared a little less. Let them judge or condemn. She had fought what was between her and Walsh, literally for years. With her divorce just two months away from being final, soon nothing would stop them from being together openly and happily.

Kerris was hunting through a pile of scarves for one that would work with the dress a customer had found when the noise in the shop slowly petered out until the room was eerily quiet for six o'clock in the evening.

"Mrs. Peterson, what about this one?" Kerris's voice rang out in the unnaturally quiet shop. "Think this one will work?"

She laid the floral scarf against the dress Mrs. Peterson was wearing, and looked up to gauge her reaction. But Mrs. Peterson wasn't looking at Kerris. Her eyes clung to the shop entrance over Kerris's shoulder. Matter of fact, that's where everyone's attention seemed focused.

Kerris glanced around, doing a double take when she spotted Walsh, filling the doorway with his broad shoulders and imposing height. He wore a white Walsh Foundation T-shirt, stark against his tanned skin, and his standard-issue cargo pants. He surveyed the shop, and his eyes stopped as soon they met hers. His wide, warm smile and the heat in his eyes melted Kerris like the sun on an ice cap. He walked into the shop, ignoring the curiosity of the customers tracking his every step. Yes, he was handsome, but he was also Walsh Bennett. His family was like royalty in this town, and these people followed his moves in the tabloids and on blogs. Kerris actually saw one woman aim her phone his way and snap a picture.

He grabbed her hand as soon as he was close enough, pulling her to his side and dropping a quick kiss into her hair. Kerris stiffened under everyone's inspection. They all knew who she was. Who Walsh was. Who Cam was. How had she fooled herself into believing she didn't care what they thought? In that moment, as much as she had missed Walsh and wanted nothing more than to leap into his arms, legs wrapped around waist à la Whitney-loves-Bobby-Brown-fresh-from-jail, she couldn't. She put a step between them, gently tugging her hand free.

"Hi, Walsh." She offered a careful smile, her eyes pleading with him to follow her lead. "What a nice surprise. We weren't expecting you."

Walsh tilted his head and raised one dark brow.

"I tried to stay away," Walsh said, voice deliberately loud. "But I missed you too much."

Self-consciousness forced her to meet one curious set of eyes after another around the shop. These women had thrown her a baby shower. Kerris had helped them find dresses for special occasions and gifts for the people they loved. They had brought casseroles, magazines, and trashy novels to her home when she was confined to a wheelchair for months. In many ways, they were extended family, and though Kerris knew she would choose Walsh no matter what, a part of her wanted them to approve.

"Well, I think the two of you make the sweetest couple," Mrs. Peterson said into the waiting quiet.

Kerris looked from the scarf she still held to the compassion in the other woman's eyes.

"Thank you, Mrs. Peterson," Kerris managed to say.

"It's obvious you two belong together," Mrs. Peterson said, extending her hand to Walsh. "Dorthea Peterson, I've been coming to the shop since it opened. I knew your mother, God rest her soul. She was an amazing woman. We all miss her."

Walsh nodded and offered Mrs. Peterson a genuine smile. He didn't look at Kerris, but the tight jaw and clenched fist he slid into his pocket signaled that he wasn't altogether pleased with her.

"Thank you. I miss her, too."

"I heard your father is holding a big shindig in her honor up there in New York." Another customer, the one with the camera phone, said from across the room.

Walsh turned in the woman's direction, another smile on his face.

"Yes, ma'am. It's for an endowment in my mother's name Bennett Enterprises has created."

"In two weeks, right?"

"Yes." Walsh lifted impressed eyebrows. "You're well informed."

The customer looked a little sheepish.

"We all keep up with your family. You've done a lot for this community."

Another smile from Walsh and then his eyes drifted back to Kerris. She hated to see the smile he'd held on to for everyone else wither and die when his eyes landed on her. He didn't speak, but just let the quiet build between them like a brick wall. Just as she was about to say something, probably the wrong thing, Meredith joined them.

"Walsh, good to see you." Meredith slapped Walsh on the arm and brought him in for a hug, giving Kerris WTF eyes around his shoulder.

Kerris was asking herself WTF. She'd been mooning over this man all day, waiting for a phone call, and he shows up in the beautiful flesh and she messes it up this badly?

"You look great, Mer." Walsh tweaked the hair spiking around her gamine face. "I like the pink."

"You know me. Always trying something new." Meredith turned to Kerris. "I've got things handled out here, Ker."

"Oh, um. Okay." Kerris turned to Walsh, her face a silent question he refused to answer. "Would you like to…we could…if you want…"

Walsh didn't acknowledge the word salad Kerris couldn't stop tossing. He walked past her and toward the back office. Meredith slammed her palm against her forehead and shooed Kerris after him.

"Go fix that," Meredith whisper-shouted.

Kerris wasn't sure how to fix whatever she had broken. Once in the office, she leaned against the door, unsure what to do with her hands. If she hadn't botched things up so badly, she'd already be in Walsh's arms. Against a wall getting the sense kissed out of her. This was not the reunion she had envisioned.

"I um…" Kerris cleared her throat. "I wasn't expecting you. I thought you were in meetings all day in New York and wouldn't be back until the weekend."

Walsh crossed his arms, molding the shirt to the hardness of his chest. "I wanted to see you and had Trish clear my schedule."

"I'm glad you're here."

"I wouldn't have known it by how you dropped my hand out there and stepped away from me in front of everyone like I had the plague." His eyes, marble hard, didn't leave her face. "What was that, Kerris?"

"I didn't mean to do that." She pressed herself deeper into the door, wishing she could blend into the paneling. "It was a knee-jerk response. I just don't want people to think we are—"

"But we are." Walsh ran hands through his hair, a little longer than when she had last seen him. "Aren't we?"

"Of course. I don't want people judging us."

"And I honestly don't care."

"I don't want Cam hearing about us through the grapevine or some blog or tabloid."

"Baby, even if Cam hasn't heard anything, he knows. Our being together was an eventuality he has been preparing himself for since he left." He pointed to the door that was her support. "That out there? You treated me like a friend."

"I just wasn't prepared for you to show up. I'm sorry. What do you want me to do?"

Walsh pushed off the desk and strode over to stand in front of her, caging her in with his arms on either side of her against the door.

"I want you to claim me." He touched the orchid charm hanging just outside the rounded collar of her dress. "The same way I claim you every time we're in a room together."

And he always did. Kisses, holding her hand, wrapping her in his arms. Even every look was a claim he staked on her. It probably always had been.

"For so long, I couldn't claim you, Kerris. I couldn't look at you. I couldn't kiss you or touch you. You weren't *mine*." He slid his fingers into the hair at the back of her neck. "Now you are and I want everyone to know."

"But I'm also still married to your best friend."

"He's not my best friend anymore, and I don't care if someone blogs that we're together, tweets it, takes pictures of it, puts it on a damn billboard. Good. Then the whole world will know where we stand."

"You don't have to live in this small town where everybody knows everybody and has opinions about everything. I don't want to humiliate Cam. I don't want to disrespect him, and I don't want to be the one everyone's talking about."

"You don't have to live here either."

"What? Of course I do."

"Not if you come live with me in New York."

"Have you heard anything I've said?"

"Yeah, I just don't care." He smiled for the first time since she had entered the room. "Okay, I do care how you feel, and I'm willing to wait for you to move to New York."

"Thank you."

"But I want you there with me in two weeks."

"Two weeks?"

She already knew. Had seen this coming and had been bracing herself for it.

"To the fund-raiser my dad is hosting in New York. I want you with me."

Kerris gulped back her irrational fear. Slapped down the lies about her inadequacy and inferiority. For years all they'd had was stolen looks and the loneliness of their imaginations. It was one thing to go out for dinner here, or to take a walk through River-mont Park. Most of the time when he was here, they wanted to be alone anyway and stayed on the houseboat, which Walsh had bought for them to have some privacy. New York was Walsh's home turf, the biggest stage in the world. The media took pictures of Walsh doing something as mundane as grabbing coffee in the morning. Imagine what they'd do with a story as twisted around and convoluted as theirs and Cam's.

"Baby, I'm waiting." Walsh dipped his head until he was level with her. His eyes were free of anger and frustration, and had started fogging with familiar hunger. "I really want to be done with this so I can kiss you."

Kerris tilted up on her toes, aiming for his mouth. He turned his head at the last minute, looking back for confirmation.

"Not yet. Will you come with me to the fund-raiser? In New York? In front of everyone?"

He didn't say it aloud, but his eyes asked the question.

Will you claim me?

She looked at his handsome face, the intense green eyes she lost herself in if she wasn't careful. The tender hands even now stroking along her neck and caressing her collarbone. She couldn't deny him anything. She couldn't deny him—period.

"Will you come?" He asked again, hovering over her mouth, hands already pushing up her dress and squeezing her butt.

She was losing her mind wanting him, but before she capitulated and gave in to the storm that always broke between them, she gave him the answer he wanted.

"I'll come."

He gave her his devilish grin, gripping her thigh with one hand and sliding the other into her panties.

"That's always music to my ears."

Chapter Nineteen

Two weeks later, Kerris looked around the marbled, tiered space in the Metropolitan Museum of Art and reminded herself these were all just people. Beautifully dressed, wealthy people from esteemed families, who had attended all the right schools, but just people. At least she had the beautifully dressed part covered.

When Kerris confessed to Walsh how nervous she was about what to wear, the last person she had expected to show up unannounced on her doorstep for a shopping spree was Jo. Their relationship had definitely gotten better since they'd talked things out at Christmas, but Kerris hadn't been dating Walsh then, so she wasn't sure what to expect.

Kerris had been unprepared for the near-military approach Jo took to shopping. Jo had marched through New York City like General Sherman, and Kerris felt like the spoils of war right about now. Jo had plotted their course up and down Madison Avenue. With a Bennett car at their disposal, they ran through a blur of exclusive shops Kerris could barely recollect. Her mind was like a fashion-challenged sieve that couldn't hold on to all the label names Jo had flung at her.

Euphoric with Walsh's Black Card burning an outfit-sized hole in her Bottega Veneta, Jo loved several things at Bergdorf, a couple of things at Henri Bendel, and one thing each at Barneys and Calvin Klein. Kerris, on the other hand, felt overwhelmed by everything she tried on. As much as she hoped it wouldn't be the case, she suspected tonight would be her introduction to New York society as Walsh Bennett's girlfriend. She wanted to get it just right, and nothing had been just right until she'd found the outfit she was currently second-guessing.

The reality of wearing such a daring ensemble out in public was much different from the idea of it. She felt men's eyes on her and wondered if she'd made a terrible mistake.

A black jumpsuit of satin crepe, its minuscule straps practically invisible, it gave the illusion that the whole thing was suspended and held up by magic. There was no waistline, but it skimmed her curves in such a way that emphasized the narrowness of her waist and the flare of her hips. The legs slouched before tapering at the calf. The rear view left her bare down to the small of her back, dipping dramatically and dangerously close to the upper swells of her backside. Added to it were Kerris's first Louboutins, which Jo treated like a rite of passage, and a leopard print Alexander McQueen clutch.

"I'm only going to say this once and if you tell anyone I said it, I will deny it." Jo swept her eyes from Kerris's perfectly piled-up hair to her extravagantly shod feet. "You were right and I was wrong about that outfit. You look amazing."

"You sure it's not too much?"

"Too much what?"

"Too revealing?"

"Let's just say I guarantee Walsh will like it."

Kerris wasn't too sure. She pulled at the nonexistent back of the jumpsuit, trying to cover some of the naked skin she was flashing.

"Stop fidgeting," Jo said from beside her. "You look nervous."

"I *am* nervous." Kerris bit her thumbnail.

"Are you biting a nail?" Jo flicked horrified eyes from the offending finger to Kerris's face. "Why don't you just send everyone a group text saying you don't think you're good enough for Walsh Bennett?"

"Jo, it's not that." Though on some level it might be a little. "I'm just not used to being in these environments."

"Well, you better get used to it." Jo looked over the glittering gallery of the Met. "This is Walsh's world, and he wants you in it."

Why? Kerris hated that that was her first thought. When would she get past this soul-deep sense of not being enough? Of not deserving Walsh and all that came with him? Dr. Stein assured her that unraveling a lifetime worth of lies and destructive patterns was a process. She was right. Kerris felt very "in process" tonight, like a sojourner stumbling through a strange, affluent land with well-dressed, accomplished natives.

"Walsh and Uncle Martin will be here soon. Uncle Martin would squeeze a meeting between a wedding and a funeral if he could. I know Walsh would have preferred to come with you himself." Jo's matte red lips were dramatic against her creamy skin and dark hair. "I want you out of this state of…whatever it is by the time he gets here."

"I'm trying, Jo."

Kerris looked up at the woman who seemed to have it all. Only Kerris knew that what Jo wanted most, she might never hold. Cam. For some reason, that knowledge helped Kerris. If a total package like Jo had a fifteen-year unrequited love in her closet, maybe everyone had something to wrestle with. Maybe her demons were just that. Hers. And everyone else, no matter how many zeroes they harbored in their checking accounts, had theirs.

"Look, I don't really understand all the self-esteem issues you have or the abandonment crap you've bought into over the years. Sorry." Jo's tough-girl eyes softened and she quirked her mouth. "You want to know why I don't understand it? I don't get it because you are the most beautiful girl in this room. You are one of the most giving and sweet people I've ever met. I've known most of these girls most of my life, and I'd pick you over every one of them for Walsh."

Stunned didn't cover it. After the resentment Jo had expressed on more than one occasion since "the kiss," even their last amiable conversation hadn't prepared Kerris for that response.

"Wow, Jo. I don't know what to say."

"That's probably for the best." Jo smoothed her hands over her one-shouldered Hervé Léger bandage dress. The saleswoman had called the color alabaster. "Girls usually say stupid shit in moments like these."

For a heartbeat, Kerris wasn't sure how to take it, but Jo's twitching lips gave her away. The twitch turned into a full-on guffaw and Jo, whom Walsh and Cam had more than once called "queen," bent over laughing, arms folded over her trim waist. Not regal at all.

"Kerris, you should see your expression right now."

Jo's pretty face lit up with the laughter she couldn't seem to stop. One moment Kerris wondered if Jo was hysterical and in need of a good slap, and the next she was laughing with her unstoppably, too. And for the first time, Kerris understood why Walsh and Cam would do anything for this girl. Why she was the rock. In the midst of a mini-meltdown, Jo had managed to make Kerris realize how silly holding on to her fears and reservations was. Had made her laugh uncontrollably when moments before she'd wanted to skulk off to the ladies' room and hide in a stall.

"You're good people, Jo."

Jo slowly sobered, but her face held on to a mischievous grin.

"Don't tell anyone, okay?" Jo's smile fell away altogether. "Walsh is here."

"Where?" Kerris scanned the room, looking for the proud dark head and wide shoulders.

Jo nodded her head in the direction just over Kerris's shoulder. "He's over there."

Kerris started to turn around, only to have Jo grab her elbow.

"Don't turn around. Don't look."

"Well, how am I going to—" Kerris stood perfectly still, as if one movement would shatter something fragile. "Tell me what to do."

"Okay, he's got company, and he won't be able to get away for a while, if I'm guessing correctly." Jo cast a discreet glance across the room. "He's with the chairman of the Bennett board of directors, Paul Garrison. Sofie's father, Ernest Baston, is over there, too. He's Uncle Martin's business partner. And Sofie's with them. She *is* the foundation's goodwill ambassador, but I just didn't think about her being here."

Kerris's blood congealed in her veins to a slow chug. This night was becoming a tape on rewind. Here she was again as the misfit Cinderella, dressed in unfamiliar finery, surrounded by a rarefied

colony of people who had been reared to rule. And the queen of
the ball was once again standing with the man she wanted.

"This is it, Kerris."

"This is what?"

"I know these people look nice, and some of them are. But
your man? He is the ultimate prize, honey, and you are swimming
in a shark tank tonight. Be on the offensive. Don't wait to defend
your territory."

"Are we still talking about me and Walsh?"

"Sweetie, we never stopped." Jo mixed just enough compassion
with the grit in her voice. "You are going to walk over there and
show all these bitches why he chose you."

But what if she still didn't know why herself?

I want you to claim me.

Walsh had said it, and his words massaged the last knots from
her composure, centering her. Reminding her of the peace she
found when she was with him. Of the rightness no one could take
from them, if she didn't let them.

"Okay, I'll tell you when to turn—"

Jo stopped mid-sentence because Kerris had already turned.

She said over her shoulder, "Thanks, Jo. I think I got it."

She looked back at the beautiful girl, who reminded her of
Kristeene the more time she spent with her. "Thanks for everything."

Jo gave her a quick grin and a thumbs-up.

Kerris headed in the direction of the small group clustered
around Walsh. She saw the two men Jo had mentioned. She
could actually see traces of Sofie's Nordic beauty in the tall man
nursing a glass of champagne. The shorter gentleman must be
the chairman of the board. And then there was Sofie. Her long
red nails lay on Walsh's arm. She reminded Kerris of a gorgeous

python, trying to wrap any part of herself she could around Walsh, and Kerris watched as he kept discreetly pulling away. He turned, and Kerris walked toward his back. Sofie looked up at him and over his shoulder. She saw Kerris first, and her green eyes went glacial. The wide, soft mouth stiffened into a frozen line.

Kerris walked up behind Walsh and slowly, surely slipped her hand into his. He looked annoyed for a moment and her heart fell. Then she realized he thought it was Sofie again. As soon as he saw her, his face transformed.

"Hey. I was looking for you." He didn't kiss her, but his eyes went thermal as they scoured all the bare surfaces of her body, sending feathers floating in her belly. She wished they were alone and he could peel the jumpsuit right off her.

"I was with Jo and saw you come in."

She squeezed his hand, then lifted up onto her toes until she could reach his mouth. And in front of all the sharks, and with her eyes wide open and holding his, settled a kiss on his mouth, soft and certain. Walsh's grin widened and he wrapped an arm around her waist before turning to face the other two men. Kerris could feel their curiosity, along with everyone else's in the immediate vicinity, pique.

"Paul, Ernest, I don't believe you've met my girlfriend, Kerris Moreton."

Kerris ignored Sofie, who was choking on her champagne, and extended her hands to both men.

"So nice to meet you." Kerris said, leaning into Walsh's side.

"Kerris came through the foundation's scholarship program," Walsh said, pride coloring his voice and warming his eyes when he looked at her.

For the first time Kerris realized what an accomplishment he considered it. That she had worked hard and propelled herself into a future of her own making. She hadn't grown up with the grooming or the opportunities most people in this room had, but she had made the most of every chance.

"Yes." Kerris gave her smile and full attention to Walsh, wanting this moment for them. "Kristeene interviewed me herself."

"And she loved you," Walsh said, his eyes as fixed on hers as hers were on him. "You were always one of her favorites. If not her favorite."

"Surely her favorite would have been Cam," Sofie said, interjecting for the first time, her perfect white teeth camouflaging the fangs Kerris knew lay behind them. "Have you met Cam, Paul? He's Kerris's husband."

Had the music stopped? Had all conversations ceased? Sofie's voice fell into sudden quiet, and it seemed the silence swelled with the curiosity of everyone within hearing distance.

"Sofie," Ernest Baston rebuked, his eyes uncomfortable as they shifted between Walsh and Kerris.

"Well, he is her husband, Daddy." Sofie took a swig of her champagne, but Kerris knew the other woman was nowhere near drunk. She knew exactly what she was doing. "Not like I made that up."

Walsh's hand tightened around Kerris's fingers and he cleared his throat. Kerris knew he was about to defend her. Make excuses. Anything to save face. For her. Because she knew he didn't give an actual damn what anyone thought.

And now, neither did she.

"Sofie's right, of course," Kerris said before Walsh could start. "I am married to Cam, but we've been separated for more than a year. Our divorce will be final soon."

Kerris looked back to Walsh, layering meaning in her voice that she hoped he heard.

"He's a very good friend to both Walsh and me, and we wish him only the best."

Walsh brought her fist to his lips and nodded.

"Kerris is right. Cam is a great friend to us both." Walsh spread his grin around to everyone but Sofie. "Now what were you gentlemen saying about the sheikh? I need all the pointers I can get."

Sofie huffed a disgusted breath and stalked off toward the restrooms. Oh, no. Not this time.

"Walsh, I'll be back."

He paused to cast a worried look in Sofie's direction.

"Baby, maybe you should—"

She reached up until she could pour the words in his ear without anyone else hearing.

"Now it's time for *you* to trust *me*."

She pulled back and raised her brows, silently asking permission to go after the woman who had, in many ways, been such a thorn in her side. He brushed his fingers across the orchid charm she wore.

"Okay, but hurry back. I want to show you off."

Kerris gripped the charm between her fingers as she walked, growing more confident the closer she got to the bathroom. Kerris saw Ardis, Rivermont's mayor's daughter and Sofie's friend, as soon as she entered. Both she and Sofie were freshening their makeup in the mirror, and again Kerris felt like this night was a do-over cosmic joke. This had happened before. Only it had been Kristeene Bennett's birthday. Kerris had huddled in a stall, hiding from her feelings for Walsh and wrestling with her answer to Cam's proposal. And these girls had talked about her like she was not much of anything. Sofie had said Walsh would marry her.

Kerris looked at Ardis, not even bothering to smile.

"Would you excuse us…Ardis, isn't it?"

"I don't have to leave." Ardis settled onto the counter, defiance painted on her face along with the heavy makeup. "If we—"

"Get out, Ard." Sofie's eyes never left her own reflection in the mirror as she ran her hands through her trademark silver-blond hair.

Once Ardis left, Kerris wasn't sure what to do with the lying, narcissistic bag of model bones in front of her.

"You wanted me, so here I am." Sofie turned from the mirror, facing Kerris for the first time. Her eyes weren't hard. They were hot and angry. "What the fuck do you want, little maid?"

There was a time when this woman's words had cut her down, had reiterated all the lies Kerris had told herself and bought lock, stock, and barrel all her life. But something had changed. Was it Dr. Stein, excavating her hurts? Was it Walsh's unconditional, enduring love? She'd been unsure that she was ready for this alien planet of plenty Walsh occupied, but she would go wherever he went. She would hold her own against the bitches Jo had said were out there. And certainly against this bitch in the bathroom.

"You lied that night." Kerris knew she was starting in the middle, but Sofie was a bright girl. She'd catch up. "The night of Kristeene's birthday party, you said Walsh told you he'd marry you soon."

"Is that why you—" Sofie folded her long, willowy body in half, laughter shaking her slim shoulders. "Did you go off and get engaged because of *that*?"

Sofie laughed so hard she finally stumbled to a bench against a wall.

"What kind of idiot..." More cackling. "Honey, I knew you were in that stall by your little Goodwill shoes. I had no idea I was the cause of all this trouble. You truly are a stupid girl."

Kerris invaded Sofie's space, leaning in until their noses nearly touched.

"I was stupid to believe a conniving bitch like you, Sofie, but the mark of a smart girl?" Kerris straightened, walking over to the mirror to adjust the pins securing her hair in an elaborate up-sweep. "We learn from our mistakes. I must have done something right because I'm walking away with Walsh Bennett."

"Why, you little nobody." Sofie curled her petal pink lips, lunging forward even though she remained seated.

"This nobody is marrying Walsh Bennett." Kerris turned to face the nemesis she hadn't even really known was her enemy all these years.

Sofie swallowed and narrowed her eyes at Kerris. For the first time she looked pathetic. An angry girl with sad, hard-as-emerald eyes who probably hadn't eaten a decent meal in the last five years. Pathetic.

"That night you said you'd marry Walsh Bennett and have his babies." Kerris walked to the door, turning to give Sofie one last glance over her bare shoulder. "But I'm going to actually do that. Unlike you, I'm not making it up."

Sofie sat there unmoving, something close to shock on her face. She reminded Kerris of a viper who'd been bitten and felled by a bunny rabbit, and still couldn't quite believe it.

"Nothing to say?" Kerris asked. "Well, I need to get back out there. It's kind of a big night for us. Enjoy the rest of the evening. I hear there's steak."

Chapter Twenty

You sure you're okay?" Walsh asked Kerris a fourth time, watching her eat her steak and snow peas like she hadn't just emerged unscathed from a death match with Sofie in the ladies' room.

"Why wouldn't I be?" Kerris took a bite of her potatoes. "Mmmm. These are delicious, baby. You got shafted with the cauliflower. Taste."

She held her fork to his lips, waiting for him to open and sample. He complied, watching her warily like at any moment she would jerk the fork back and pretend they weren't even together. She had been amazingly at ease all night. He loved it and just hoped it lasted.

"Remind me never to send you out shopping with my cousin again." Walsh ran hungry eyes over Kerris's naked back in the jumpsuit that had him and probably every man at the table hard as cement. "You look…we'll talk later, when I can *show* you how I feel about the way you look."

As confident as she had been all night, a little color swiped her cheeks. He, Walsh Bennett, had actually ended up with a girl who still blushed. Minor miracle.

"I think I'll skip dessert and have you instead. I can't get enough of you."

"We have this whole week in New York." Her smile was made of fairy tales and shooting stars, all the things people teach you not to believe in. But here she sat. Real. His.

"We do have this week, but I leave for Tokyo Sunday."

"Tokyo?" He heard as much disappointment in her voice as he'd felt when his dad told him earlier.

"Yeah, I just found out today." He touched a renegade curl that had escaped her updo. "Only for ten days."

"It's fine."

He leaned closer, discreetly nuzzling the spot behind her ear.

"It's not fine. I ache when I'm away from you."

He ran his fingers down the fragile chain of vertebrae in her back. He leaned in, brushing her lips with his, never breaking the stare that kept them joined by an invisible, sensual thread. She swallowed his groan at the brief contact, gripping the sleeve of his well-cut sports coat.

"Am I really going to have to ask you two to get a room?" Jo asked from the seat beside him. He'd forgotten his cousin was even at the table. He'd forgotten everyone except Kerris.

"Sorry." Walsh held Kerris's hand on his knee.

"No need to apologize," Uncle James said from the seat across the table. "Young love."

Walsh searched Unc's face for any sign of judgment. His uncle hadn't approved of how things had unfolded with Cam, but ever since Walsh told him about his relationship with Kerris and that he intended to marry her, the older man had been nothing but supportive.

"Mom would be proud of Dad for this endowment Bennett is funding, huh?" he asked his uncle.

Uncle James looked down at his plate, nodding to himself before looking back to Walsh. "She'd be very proud. So am I."

Walsh considered the range of emotions he'd ever experienced toward his father. Everything from hate to indifference. This emotion was new.

"Yeah, I'm proud of him, too."

"Maybe you can tell him sometime." Uncle James grinned as Martin Bennett walked up to the table.

"Well, I see you finally got her, son."

"Dad, you obviously remember, Kerris. Kerris, my dad, Martin Bennett."

"Oh, yes, we've met." Martin took Kerris's hand. "Not under the best circumstances the last time, huh, young lady?"

"I never got the chance to thank you for bringing Walsh home."

"It was touch and go there for a minute." Martin looked at Walsh and grinned. "Hopefully, my son won't hoard your company, though neither of us is known for sharing. He's already told me he's holding you hostage this week."

"A willing hostage." She looked down at the table for a moment when both men laughed.

"Delightful." Martin shared a knowing look with his son. "Hostile takeover, huh?"

"I don't know who's been taken over." Walsh glanced over at Kerris. "But it doesn't really matter anymore."

"So it's like that?" Martin Bennett asked, raising one eyebrow.

"Oh, it's definitely like that. As soon as some loose ends are tied up."

"Loose ends. Is that what you call him?" Martin laughed. "I'm being signaled that it's time. I'd better get up there. Sorry you have to sit through this speech, Kerris."

As proud as Walsh was of his father and as excited as he was about the Bennett endowment benefiting his mother's favorite causes, impatience chafed him for the rest of the night. There was only one thing he wanted now. Only one place he wanted to be. Alone with Kerris.

In their new home.

Chapter Twenty-One

Kerris fought sleep, dropping her head to Walsh's shoulder as they whizzed through the streets on their way to his place. She could get used to being driven around everywhere in a limousine if it meant snuggling like this.

She'd seen a side of Martin Bennett that night she had only suspected existed when she met him the first time. He had surprised her and most of the people in the room when he talked openly about his ex-wife's lost battle with cancer, and the lessons she had taught him about giving back. He'd looked at Walsh, adding that his son had continued his education last summer in Kenya.

"Your father isn't at all like I imagined him, like everyone said he is."

"He's changed a lot since Mom passed." Walsh brushed one strong hand across her hair. "But he's still Martin Bennett under it all. Don't be fooled."

She opened her eyes long enough to tease him. "And are you still Walsh Bennett under it all?"

"Yeah, that's who you're stuck with," he said, his face more serious than her teasing comment called for.

She perked up when she saw the humor vacate the rugged lines of his face.

"Walsh, what's wrong?"

"Nothing's wrong." He took her hand in his, studying her in the light provided by the city. "I'm just a lot like my dad, especially when it comes to getting what I want. I'm not sure you'll like it."

"I like *you*."

"That's good because, like I said, you're stuck with me." He paused before saying the next words as if he were weighing each one before it left his mouth. "When my dad retires, if the board doesn't think I can do the job, they'll find a way for me not to do the job. There are men older than me who've been at Bennett longer than I have, who feel they have just as much right to it as I do. And in many ways they're right. Except it's mine."

The possessive word hung in the air between them. And Kerris could practically see the strands of DNA Walsh's father had passed on to him.

"My father built that company from nothing, and he wants a Bennett running it when he's done. And that'll be me. Make no mistake about it."

"Are you trying to scare me? Nothing you've said makes me love you less."

"I don't want to scare you. I want you to know me and to love me in spite of the parts of me that aren't always good."

"Oh, you mean the way you love me."

"Baby, I love you every way there is." He gently bit the curving bow of her top lip.

"We're here."

"This is your place?" She'd envisioned an apartment in the heart of the city. A high rise. Shiny, glass, doorman. This was a townhome. Three stories. Large and imposing, but charming. "Where are we?"

"TriBeCa. And, no, it's not my apartment. It's the house where I grew up. Well, at least until my parents divorced."

"You live here? But I thought—"

"It's a recent development. Come on."

It was spacious, yet homey. Luxurious, yet quaint.

"It's empty," she said.

"For now. I was hoping...well, I was hoping you'd help me fill it."

Fill it? With what? Furniture? Laughter? Love? Children? Where had all the bravado she'd shown Sofie gone? Miss "I'm Marrying Walsh Bennett" almost lost her dinner as soon as he mentioned a future. She had to make it through divorce court before she could even entertain "filling" this house with anything. She feigned interest in the gleaming hardwood floors.

"These are beautiful." She deliberately didn't look at him, provoking a deep, amused rumble from his broad chest.

"Yes, they're great floors." He lifted her chin to look at him instead of the hardwoods, a small smile on his face. "Baby, that wasn't a proposal."

Her shoulders dropped with a little relief and a little disappointment.

He took her left hand, stroking the ring finger with his thumb.

"You'll know when I'm proposing." He kissed her empty finger. "Let me show you your room."

They mounted the stairs and turned left. Walsh gestured to the right.

"The room I slept in growing up is that way," he said. "You'll be in my parents' old room."

"Oh, no, Walsh, you should have the master. I don't want to put you out."

"Do you honestly think I'm gonna sleep down the hall with you here?"

"Maybe I'll lock you out!"

She took off running, and he chased her.

"You don't even know which room it is." He laughed behind her.

Kerris skittered down the hall in her precipitous heels, jerking open the first door she came to, dashing in only to skid to a stop. It was a huge bedroom with a large bed at its center. The far wall was made almost entirely of glass, providing a glorious view of the city's distant skyline. She walked over to the window, pressing her palm flat to the glass. The city really was captivating. She thought of Rivermont, with its quaint shops, busybodies, and the river as its pulsing, life-giving heart. She wished she could live in two places at once, inhabit two worlds.

"It's beautiful." She heard the wistful note in her own voice.

"You took the words." Walsh walked up behind her, feathering kisses down her neck, skimming her bare spine with his fingers. "Don't wear this again."

Her breath came in short gasps from the steam his mouth and fingers stoked inside of her. He squatted behind her, possessing the small of her back with his mouth, running his tongue over the base of her spine, licking between the bones.

"I thought you liked it."

"Me and every other man at the Met tonight." He rose to his

full height, liberating her hair from the pins until it flooded his hands. "I thought I was gonna have to knock some heads together before the night was over."

Walsh pulled the almost nonexistent straps from her shoulders with his teeth. He scooped his big hands under her arms, lifting her until they were eye to eye. He plunged into her mouth, hungry, seeking, ravishing. Kerris clawed her fingers around his head, clutching him closer, deeper. She felt the cool slide of the silky material against her skin when it finally succumbed to the laws of physics and gravity, pooling on the floor beneath her feet. Walsh held her suspended in the air. He laid her down on the huge bed, locking eyes with her before he discovered her body with worshipping hands—like Magellan or Columbus, exploring a glorious new world, but one of flesh and delicate bone. He licked at the beauty mark above her right breast, a drop of dark chocolate in the silkiest honeyed cream of her skin.

"I never tire of this." The emotion simmering in Walsh's eyes sent a wave of heat and then a shiver along her bare skin. "Of tasting you."

Kerris's hands, urgent and seeking, pushed the jacket away from his shoulders, glorying in the width, the breadth, of him. She pulled at the buttons of his shirt, forcing her fingers to slow even as her breath came in short pants.

He laved the velvety curve of her neck with his tongue, anointing the skin with gentle bites that had her writhing beneath him as they devoured each other's mouths and frantically explored each other's bodies. Her clothes long discarded, chest heaving, Kerris wrapped her legs around his and pushed into him, only his slacks separating her from what she needed more than air. She was hollow. She was an empty ache without him. It wasn't enough.

"Walsh, oh God. Inside. I need you inside."

"Kerris." He pushed her name out, ragged between harsh breaths. He pressed his forehead to hers. "We have to stop. Baby, we can't."

"Yes, we can." She bit his earlobe with delicate ferocity.

"They're your ground rules. You didn't want to do that to him."

Him. Cam.

The name poured ice water on her passion, the steam of shame and guilt rising up off her heated flesh. She sat up, grabbing for the edge of the richly colored duvet, pulling it over her bare breasts.

"Oh, God, Walsh." Embarrassment watered her voice. "I just…I forgot. I didn't mean…I didn't want…"

"I wanted." He collapsed onto his back, arm flung across his eyes. She heard the deliberate slowing of his breath. "I still want."

"I'm glad you stopped." Kerris wished she'd had the willpower and presence of mind to. "You could have…well, I wouldn't have stopped you."

"As much as I want you, it wouldn't have been worth your guilt. And I know you would've felt guilty."

How many men would think like that?

"You're right. I would have felt awful if it came up in the divorce hearing. If they asked if we…you know…actually had sex, and I had to say we'd…well, you know."

"Divorce hearing?" Walsh lowered his arm from his eyes to look at her. "When is that?"

"Less than a month away."

"Will Cam be there?" Kerris heard the strain in his voice.

"Yeah, I guess so." Kerris tightened her fingers around the cover concealing her naked breasts, working up the nerve to ask a question she had considered more than once. "Do you ever miss him?"

"Doesn't matter." Walsh started sitting up, but Kerris pushed him back down.

"Do you?" She leaned over him and searched his eyes for the truth.

"Sometimes, I guess." His eyes held hers for a few moments before he looked at some point over her shoulder. His eyes turned flinty. "It doesn't matter."

"Walsh, one day—"

"Let's get something straight." Walsh carefully removed her hand and dragged himself to sit with his back against the headboard. "The only one day I care about is ours. Yours and mine."

"I don't want you to wake up someday resenting me for taking away someone who was such a huge part of your life."

"He left you, abandoned you."

"He left Mama Jess with me."

"Are you defending him?"

"No, but I'm not defending myself either. Jo told me about the fight." Kerris swallowed, not knowing details, but knowing how barbed Cam's tongue could be. And knowing Walsh.

"What fight?" Walsh stood up and walked to the end of the bed, leaning one shoulder against the bedpost, eyes hedging.

"Between you and Cam." She crawled to the end of the bed, carefully clutching the covers around herself. She looked up at him. "I know it's not easy thinking about his time with me." She reached for his hand.

"You mean about him having sex with you?" His face like granite, Walsh clenched his other hand into a tight fist.

"Yeah, I guess." She squeezed a small breath into the narrowed passage of her lungs. "I know this is awkward."

"It's wrong that he had you, and that I...God, if you had only listened to me that night, we could have—"

"Avoided all this? This is my fault, right? That's what you want to say."

She was goading him into an explosion she might regret, but at least all their cards would be on the table once and for all. He jerked his hand away, turning to lean his back against the bedpost.

"I'm not saying that. Don't put words in my mouth."

"Are you telling me that when you think about Cam with me you don't hate me just a little?" Kerris forced the words past the lump of shame clogging her throat. "Resent me just a little?"

"I could never hate you. Stop it. Don't do this."

Even with his back turned, she could see the anger calcifying his posture. He was like a famished tiger held back from raw meat by a strand of floss.

"We have only a few days together before I leave for Tokyo. I'm not wasting time talking about my feelings for Cam."

"You haven't thought about it? Haven't envisioned—"

"I said stop it right now."

Walsh turned to face her, lips clamped so tightly together the syllables were ground to paste. He strode like a caged panther to the window, facing away from her. He slammed his hand against the glass before turning back to her, the city lights behind him a beautiful spectacle.

"You should have waited, Kerris! Dammit, yes, I resented you. I had to give the toast at your fucking wedding and grin like a monkey the whole day, while my insides were torn up. I told you at the hospital we should have talked to Cam. And after what we shared in that gazebo that night, you did what? Went off and got engaged to my best friend twenty minutes later? Because you *assumed* I was marrying Sofie? What is that? Who *does* that?"

"Walsh, I—"

"No. You will damn well listen now." He shoved his hands into the pockets of his flawlessly tailored pants. He dropped the room temperature with his icy stare. "You don't poke a tiger unless you're prepared to get bitten."

She held back her words, knowing this was what she had provoked. He breathed deeply through his nostrils and out through his mouth before continuing more quietly.

"I was so angry with you." The ice in his eyes slowly thawed until only pain remained. "And I loved you so much, I loved Cam, and I wanted to do what was right, but everything felt wrong. The only thing that felt right was being with you, but I knew it wasn't right. Only because you'd made the wrong choice. It wasn't just your life. It was mine. It was Cam's. Did I resent the decision you made? I did. Do I miss Cam? I do sometimes. Do I ever, ever want to live without you again? I can't. Not ever. That's all that matters."

"But Walsh—"

"It doesn't matter what you've done, or how your choices separated us. I don't know how not to love you. And a choice between you and Cam is no choice at all."

Kerris refused to cry. She wished with all her heart that Dr. Stein were here to run interference. They needed an objective third party, a mediator, because now that she had provoked him to the ugly truth, she had no idea what to do with it. No idea what the right thing was to say, so she just said the truth that mangled her security and tugged at the threads of her assurances.

"I'm so scared it'll always haunt us." It was something she'd never even admitted to herself, that the damage she had done to his friendship, what she had cost him, would erode what he felt for her. "I'm scared that one day you'll wake up, see Cam gone and me still here, and it won't be enough and that you'll leave."

"You don't ever have to be scared of that."

"Yes, I do." She said the words with eyes closed, afraid that if she opened them, she'd lose her nerve. "Walsh, this love gives you so much power over me. Something I promised myself no one would ever have again. That I'd never be that vulnerable again. Everyone leaves."

"I won't leave you."

His tone was sure, but she was not.

"Oh, that's reassuring." Kerris's short laugh and the look she finally gave him had soaked in uncharacteristic sarcasm and bitterness. "They all leave eventually."

"Kerris, I'm not them."

"No, you're not." She balled her fists together at her waist, clenched in a nervous knot. "You're much worse. I could live with my mother splitting. And then, when I lost Mama Jess, it was like losing my mother all over again. And I knew my foster parents never loved me. And then my husband leaves me after I lost our baby. I mean, what is wrong with me that *everyone* can walk away so easily?"

"Walking away from you is impossible for me." Walsh reached for her, but came up empty when she backed out of his reach. "I'm not them."

"I know. You're not them." She knew if she unballed her hands they would shake. "Because I could live through all of them leaving. I *did* live through losing every one of them. But you...if you left me now, Walsh, it would break me in half. It would wreck me."

"I'm not going to leave you. Not ever." He caught her around the waist and pulled her to him. He stroked a steady hand down the silky fall of hair at her shoulders.

"You will." She cried into his crisp shirt. "You will, and it'll destroy me."

"Baby, I won't. I promise I won't."

"Walsh, I can't...I can't do it. I can't...if you leave me, too—"

Her words became incoherent, muddied by the sloppy tears she wept into his strong shoulder. She didn't protest when he sat on the bed and pulled her into his lap. He just held her until it seemed there could be no more tears. Kerris wondered if these were from a reservoir she'd been filling up since the day she was born. Since her mother's first leaving, which had cut so deeply—cut her to the bone. Her tears were for that original pain, and every one that had followed.

After her tears subsided, she finally sniffed, plucking at the buttons of his shirt with restless fingers. He shifted so she faced him, her legs falling on either side of his strong thighs. He pressed against her back until her breasts rested against his chest, only the duvet separating them. She clutched his shoulders, keeping the duvet aloft with only the press of their bodies together. She couldn't look at him and wondered if he could feel the gallop of her heart.

He leaned down, nudging her face up with his nose.

"Better?"

"I'm still scared." Even with everything she'd ever wanted only a breath away, her throat burned with a lifetime of tears.

"Me, too, sometimes." He pulled back, studying her wet eyes. He ran a thumb along her lashes and pressed a kiss there. "But there's nothing I can do about it. I'm yours, Kerris. Completely. There's no one else for me. Now you say it."

When she looked up into his waiting eyes, she had the sense of falling. Like something had been chasing her for a long time, and she had finally tripped, plunging forward into a blessed darkness, unsure of where she would land.

So this was love. This fear; this need. This insatiable thirst that racked her soul when she thought of him. The tremble of her hands when he was near. The catch in her breath at the thought of his hands on her body. The tenderness when she considered what an amazing man he truly was. The possessiveness that sluiced through her at even the thought of him with someone else. Was he truly hers?

"Say it, baby." The loving heat in his eyes warmed up every frigid place left by all the hurt she'd endured.

"I'm yours."

"Completely." He ran a firm hand along her back under the duvet, his hand warm against the naked flesh.

"Completely." She hovered over his mouth before leaning the last few inches, closing her lips over his and losing all sense of space. It was only them. No fear. No apprehension. No one else. And she knew that if they went down, it would be together.

Chapter Twenty-Two

Kerris glanced at her watch. She was due in court in an hour, but something had drawn her here. After almost a year of Dr. Stein urging her, encouraging her, sometimes begging her, to visit her baby's grave—she was finally doing it. It was a day to close old chapters and begin new ones. First, visit Amalie. Next, her divorce.

She would see Cam for the first time in more than a year. There had been no phone calls, texts, or emails. He had truly gone his own way in Paris. Kerris could only hope he had found as much peace as she had, but she somehow doubted it. He and Walsh were no closer to reconciling, but she had to keep trying. She had promised Ms. Kris she would bring them back together, and Kerris knew that once friendship was restored, everyone would be better off.

Her steps were tentative, but not because she wasn't sure where to go. Meredith and Mama Jess had practically drawn a map. They were both so happy she was finally taking this step. No, her feet hesitated because she wasn't sure what she would find there. Not the grave itself, but how much of herself had she buried with Amalie? Sometimes it felt like handfuls of her heart were still missing. Would this simple act of visiting the grave give any of it back? Or was that part of her heart gone forever?

She plodded her way through the cemetery, heartbeat ricocheting in her chest the closer she got. Nothing could have prepared her for what she found when she finally reached the tiny headstone with angel wings sketched in the granite.

"Cam?"

If she hadn't been so shocked to see him, she wouldn't have spoken. Would have tiptoed backward and left this first visit for another time. But seeing him, after a year, unexpectedly, and here at their daughter's grave, stole her caution. And his name had slipped out.

He looked up from where he knelt in front of the headstone. His hair, even longer than she had last seen it, dark and nearly to his shoulders, was tousled from the torture of his own fingers. His eyes, red-rimmed, held so much pain that Kerris's breath caught like she'd been punched in the throat.

He didn't get up. Didn't pretend he hadn't been weeping over their baby girl. Elbows on knees, eyes turned to the ground, he didn't speak.

"Cam, I didn't expect to see you here. I can come back later."

Kerris turned to leave but his words, low like a moan, stopped her.

"Why do I fuck everything up?"

Kerris turned back to him, hesitating only a moment before squatting beside him in front of the monument to their baby girl.

She pulled on a blade of grass, manipulating it into a tiny circle.

"We both messed up."

"But if I hadn't left the house that night, Amalie would be alive." Cam closed his eyes like he wanted to block out the world.

"And if I hadn't driven out in the rain…"

They'd said these words before to each other, and she realized neither of them had banished the guilt. She stowed the words in her head where she collected regrets and wishes and dead hopes.

"I'm sorry you never got to hold her, Kerris. She was beautiful." Cam ran his long, sensitive fingers over the headstone. "She was perfect."

They nursed a quiet between them for a few moments, both lost in their private thoughts, until Cam spoke again.

"I think about her every day."

"I do, too." Kerris worried her bottom lip between her teeth. "They say it gets easier, and in some ways it has. In other ways…"

"In other ways it feels like it keeps happening over and over again, and the pain gets no better."

"Yeah, some days it does feel like that." Kerris tossed a handful of grass away. "I wanted her so badly."

"I did, too." Cam snapped his dark brows together. "Maybe I wanted her for the wrong reasons. I thought having a family would be some kind of reset, give me some kind of clean slate. Make the past…hurt less."

"Me, too. And I thought she could save us."

"Nothing could have saved us. I see that now." Cam paused before looking at her, his eyes filled with certainty but no peace. "I saw that when I left for Paris."

"I think I knew that, too, but it still hurt when you left." Kerris's hollow laugh bounced between them in the eerie quiet. "A lot of things hurt when we were together."

Cam caressed the headstone again, swallowing and clenching the muscles in his strong jaw.

"Nothing has ever hurt like this, and I've been through some shit." He looked at her for a moment before returning to the headstone. "We both have."

Kerris wasn't sure what emboldened her to reach for Cam's hand, but she did. After all they'd been through—how he had hurt her, how she had hurt him—she expected him to flinch from her touch. He didn't. He looked into her eyes, a teary mirror of his own grief, and held on, somehow hallowing this moment between them for their baby girl. Something in that contact healed more than words. Like their hands were conductors for forgiveness, for resolution. For peace?

"Did you find any peace in Paris?"

"Pshht." Cam blew his cynicism out as a truncated breath. "I thought marrying you would bring me peace, but we just ended up adding new wounds. I thought having Amalie would bring peace, but I'm standing here in a graveyard, more fucked up than I've ever been. I'm done looking for peace, Kerris. It knows where to find me."

Kerris knew from experience that any peace she had obtained over the last year, she had relentlessly pursued. She had ripped her insides out, dumped them on the table, sorted through the hurt. It had been hard. It had been work. Peace didn't come looking for you. It sometimes hid in the pain. Sometimes camouflaged itself in the disappointments of the past, and until you looked hard enough to understand, to put it in perspective, peace could not be found. That wasn't a lesson you could relay in a conversation. You couldn't walk through that fire for anyone else. She certainly couldn't walk through it for Cam.

Kerris shifted on her haunches, legs getting stiff, and decided to stand, brushing the last of her tears away. Cam eased himself off the ground, too, wiping grass and dirt from the dark slacks he wore with a crisp white poet-collared shirt. He was dressed for court.

"So you and Walsh, huh?" Cam didn't look at her, but looked at his black boots.

"Yeah." That one word told Cam what she should have told him years ago. That she was in love with his best friend. "He's in Tokyo."

Cam nodded, and Kerris searched his eyes for bitterness and the lines of his face for anger. She didn't see those things, but what scared her was that she saw nothing else either. Cam, who had always been like a wire over water, volatile and crackling with the promise of explosion and passion, had vacant eyes. It frightened Kerris. Before she could probe, poke around the emptiness she sensed in him, he spoke again.

"We should get going. It's almost time."

He was right, and Kerris was ready to sever her ties to the past, to make her way into the future, but more than ever, with Ms. Kris's promise lodged in her heart, she was determined they would not leave Cam behind.

Chapter Twenty-Three

Well, I guess that's that." Cam opened the cottage door for Kerris. "You're a free woman."

"And you're a free man."

Kerris hoped her eyes weren't shining with the promise of her new life, but she was afraid they were. Afraid the happiness ahead for her and Walsh would be an insult to this man who had once been such a close friend to them both. The thought of seeing Walsh tomorrow literally made Kerris's heart flutter. He returned from Tokyo tonight. Ten days had turned into three weeks as negotiations dragged out. It was probably best that he and Cam weren't here at the same time.

"I just need to grab a few things from the office and I'll be outta your hair," Cam said.

"Don't rush. It's your house."

"Take your time about leaving." Cam settled onto the couch,

the line of his lips not quite committing to a smile. "I'm headed back to Paris tonight and have no plans of coming back here anytime soon."

Kerris sat on the couch across from Cam. They were newly divorced, but still had so many memories and a lot of pain looming between them, like a smear on their hearts that might not ever be wiped completely clean. Kerris hoped they'd be able to find a cleaner slate. If for no other reason than restoring the friendship that she knew, beneath all of the enmity and bitterness, both men still missed and needed. She wanted Cam in their lives. She missed the easy friendship they'd once shared before her misguided choices wrecked everything. Not just for her, but for Cam. And for Walsh.

"Cam, can I say something?"

He considered her warily from the corner of the leather couch. "What?"

"I wanted a family, a home, a future with someone I could spend my life with." Kerris ran damp palms across the pleat in her tailored slacks. "And when you offered that to me the night of the scholars dinner, knowing I couldn't love you the same way, I thought it was possible, but I was wrong."

Cam continued watching her, leaning forward and resting his elbows on his knees.

"But I don't ever want you to think I didn't love you." Kerris swallowed the lump burning a hole in her throat. "And I know you loved me. It just wasn't the love marriages are made of. We were so good as friends. I just wish we could have left it that way. I'm sorry…I'm sorry for everything."

She forced her eyes to remain glued to his, hoping the détente they had reached in the cemetery could hold through what she needed to say.

"I grabbed what you offered me with both hands and ran, thinking I could ignore or bury what I felt for Walsh. And I was doing okay with it, until he was kidnapped. That was such a scary day."

"Yeah, for me, too."

Kerris knew how important Cam and Walsh had been to each other. She just had to figure out how to get them to see it and admit it again.

"When he came home from Haiti…I don't know. We just…the walls I'd built up to protect the three of us just fell, and in that one moment, we kissed."

"Yeah, I was there for that one part." A smile tugged at the corner of Cam's mouth, and Kerris marveled not for the first time at his twisted sense of humor, a blessing and a curse.

"I felt so guilty and so broken after that. I knew I had ruined something special between the two of you, and between you and me, but I was determined to make good on the promise I made to you."

Kerris wondered, not for the first time, how she would ever keep her promise to Kristeene.

"And then I got pregnant," she said. "And I thought that was our miracle to make everything right again, but nothing was right. I was only half there, and I knew you sensed that. I'm sorry for so much."

"You may not believe it, but so am I." Cam swallowed visibly, emotion twisting his mouth until he straightened it. "What I made you do the night I saw you with Walsh—"

"Cam, don't." She couldn't talk about that. Not now. "You didn't force me."

"Didn't I?" His eyes carried the apology before he voiced it. "I'm sorry, Kerris. Sometimes I just…sometimes I'm not a good guy. Can you forgive me for that night?"

"I do." She reached across the space separating them to grip his hand. "And I know you feel guilty for leaving me after the accident. Don't. It was the best thing for all of us. I would never have been the one to leave. You saved us both by leaving. I understand that now."

"I'm glad." Cam offered her the kind of smile they hadn't shared in years. "I guess."

"Cam, we used to be friends." Kerris brushed tears away with one hand and gripped his hand harder with the other. "You remember that?"

"Yeah." Cam stood to his feet, shoving his hands deep into his pockets. "I remember."

"I want that back. I want the best for you. For you to be happy and healthy." Kerris paused, knowing the subject she needed to broach would take her toward an injured animal that might claw her flesh at any moment. "I've been seeing a therapist."

Cam narrowed his eyes at her, a warning to not go where she was about to go.

"Good for you."

"It could be good for you, too, Cam. You still have those nightmares?"

Cam raised the beautiful, dark slashes of his eyebrows.

"Oh, is this the part where you give a fuck?"

"Cam, I want you well."

"Well?" Cam's laugh boomed in the room. "Baby, I have more money than I ever imagined, can *still* get any woman I want, and am painting—living my dream. I'm more than well. I'm fucking marvelous. Trust."

"You're deflecting because you don't want me digging into this."

"Deflecting? Is that a new word your therapist taught you? Just because you've got screws loose—"

"I do have screws loose, Cam."

Kerris checked the anger she knew he was provoking to throw her off this topic even after the ground they had gained.

"I had…have…abandonment issues. Self-worth issues. And not dealing with those drove me to make bad choices, like marrying a good friend when I wasn't in love with him. Like ignoring my feelings for Walsh because I thought I wasn't good enough. My point is maybe you made some bad choices, too, because you may have…issues."

"That's your point? You can do better than that, Kerris."

"Okay, I will." Kerris held his eyes with hers, firming her mouth to say what she had realized over the course of her time with Dr. Stein. "I think you settled for what we had as much as I did because we both thought we weren't worth more. As damaged as I was, you probably thought I was the best you could do."

Horror washed away the impolite disdain Cam had so carefully held in place. Only for a moment, but long enough for Kerris to know she wasn't too far off base. Even if he didn't realize or want to admit it yet.

"Cam, get help so you can be ready for the girl who will love you the way you deserve to be loved."

Cam shook his head, something ugly twisting his beautiful face. It was hate. And it wasn't for her or for Walsh. It was for himself.

"If you still think I deserve to be loved, *you're* the one who needs help."

"Cam, our abusers—"

"Screw this. I'm getting my stuff and I'm out."

Cam turned away, walking with brisk strides toward the office.

The doorbell cut into the response she hadn't formed yet. Kerris wiped the last traces of tears from her cheeks and composed herself. She recognized that self-hatred, and knew it had less to do with anything Cam had actually done and much more to do with fundamentally who he believed himself to *be* because of the abuse he'd suffered. That lie would take a long time to untangle. In some ways, she was still untangling it herself.

Mama Jess had gone to visit her sister in the hospital after minor surgery. Meredith was at the shop. She wasn't sure who would be stopping by. When she opened the door and saw Walsh, she wanted to hurl herself at him, wrap her body around him like cellophane, but he moved first. He pulled her up and into his arms until her feet didn't touch the ground, his mouth hot and hungry against her, his tongue searching and licking heat into her with each kiss. He shifted his arms, moving one under her butt and stretching one up her back, his hand cupping her head and stroking her hair.

He pulled away long enough to whisper against her lips.

"Tell me you're free." He kissed down her chin, licking the tendon in her neck. "It's official. Tell me you're mine."

"Walsh, we should—"

"Wow, you got some balls," Cam said from behind them, just inside the house. "The ink is barely dry, and you're here already."

Kerris glanced over her shoulder, wriggling to the ground and stepping out of Walsh's arms, only to be pulled back and pressed against his chest.

"Sorry, I couldn't wait," Walsh said.

"Some things don't change," Cam said.

"Before I hid everything, buried my feelings, and didn't tell you what the hell was going on." Walsh held Cam's eyes without wavering. "And it cost me the only thing that really mattered. You and Kerris should never have gotten married."

"You're a little late to this party, dude," Cam said with wry bitterness. "We just had this conversation."

"Not with me, you didn't. I need to say this. You can be a selfish, egotistical, spoiled bastard."

"Well, this is off to a great start." Cam slid his hands into the pockets of his pants and rocked back on his heels. "Is there a 'but' coming?"

"But"—Walsh paused for emphasis—"you were the best friend I've ever had. Maybe will ever have, and I'm sorry I didn't tell you how I felt about Kerris. I'm sorry I kissed her when she was married to you, but I'm not, could *never* be, sorry that I love her or that she loves me. I'm not sure things will ever be the same between you and me—"

"Doubtful." Cam looked down at his boots.

"But I have to be honest with you this time. It's all got to be out in the open." Walsh squeezed Kerris an inch closer. She felt the heavy, frantic rhythm of his heart beat at her back. "I'm marrying Kerris."

Not a twitch. Not a blink. Kerris saw nothing on Cam's face until he drew a swift breath.

"I know that."

"Soon." Walsh reached down and around until his hand surrounded hers. "Very soon."

Chapter Twenty-Four

Walsh ignored the flicker of guilt he still felt every time he saw the man who had been his best friend. He'd never felt more ruthless. The killer instinct his father had so carefully cultivated in him over the years flared to life. There would be no doubt in Cam's mind that Kerris was his, and that Walsh intended to keep her. Walsh had allowed his feelings to be swept under a rug before, disregarded. He had watched his future taken out of his control, out of his hands. Not this time. He was in control, and he wanted every card on the table.

"Walsh, wait." Kerris stepped out of his arms and crossed over to Cam, dragging him over to stand beside Walsh.

"The last conversation I had alone with Kristeene was about the two of you." Kerris looked from one face to the other. Walsh figured his expression was about as rigidly expressionless as

Cam's. "She asked me to make a promise. That I would do everything I could to reconcile her boys."

Walsh and Cam looked away from each other. Walsh knew they both still wrestled with the grief that might always be there for his mother, the woman who had shaped both their lives so significantly.

"She died believing I would make good on that promise," Kerris continued, eyes watering and mouth trembling. "Cam, Walsh and I have both asked you to forgive us for not being honest with you when we realized how we felt. I should have faced my feelings instead of avoiding them."

Walsh watched Cam's face soften only by degrees during Kerris's speech. He had no idea how Cam was taking it.

"Cam, you've apologized for leaving after Amalie, and I understand why you did that." Kerris stood between them like a small bridge. "I forgive you. I know it's not possible to ever completely clean our slate with each other, but will you try? Will the two of you try to be…friends again?"

The two men faced each other like sparring partners, their weapons never far from reach. The betrayal, disillusion, and hurt was too deep, too real, to evaporate. Walsh glanced from Kerris's pleading face to Cam's impassive expression. Walsh remembered his mother knocking their heads together when they'd fought as adolescent boys and forcing them to apologize to each other. To make up and go back and play. It wasn't that simple anymore. He wished it were, wished that one day they could help Kerris fulfill that deathbed promise, but today wasn't that day. He could see the same regret on Cam's face.

"I think I should go." Cam's smile had been waxed on. "I left something for you in the office. Something that was yours."

"Oh. Okay." Kerris's eyes asked the question Cam obviously

wasn't going to answer. A solitary tear streaked down her cheek. "Tell me we can work this out."

"Kerris, you don't need my blessing to marry Walsh."

"It's not that." She reached for Cam's hand. "I have to make this right."

"And maybe one day, it will be." Cam's eyes reflected the same pain Walsh strained against. "For all of us. But for today, this is as right as it's gonna get. I have to meet Sebastian at the gallery. We're heading back to Paris."

"Cam, please don't leave like this." Kerris swiped at the tears still trailing down her face.

"Sweetie, this is the best I can do." Cam gave her small hand a squeeze.

"Cam, I know this is hard," Walsh said, finding it harder than he had thought it would be.

"Hard?" Cam matched the tightness in Walsh's voice. "This is more than hard. I lost my wife, my best friend, and my baby girl. It's hell."

"I'm sorry." Walsh was surprised by the hoarseness of his own voice.

"I think I believe you," Cam said, some of the bitterness flaking away from his voice. "And maybe one day that'll be enough, but not today, brother."

Kerris grabbed Cam's sleeve when he turned to leave.

"Cam, think about what I said before. Maybe talking to someone."

Cam rolled his eyes and peeled her fingers away from his arm. "No."

Without another word, he passed through the cottage door, closing it noiselessly behind him.

Kerris stared at the closed door before turning her concern on Walsh.

"I'm worried about him."

"Cam's a survivor. He'll be fine. Eventually."

"But Walsh, he needs help. He—"

"Baby, the same way we have to sort our own shit out, so does he. We've done all we can do to make our part up to him, short of not being together. And that's not going to happen, so we wait."

He pulled her into his arms, drawing his first clear breath since he'd left for Tokyo.

"When he's ready, we'll be there for him. If he'll let us."

"You want that?" She rested her hand on his shoulder. "To reconcile with him?"

"I don't know." He gave her his real answer. "What I do know is that I didn't come here to talk about Cam."

"Really? Is that so?" The look she offered teased him, but Walsh couldn't laugh. Couldn't even force himself to smile, because the weight of the next few moments pressed into his chest until his heart hurt.

"I want to tell you a story." Walsh steadied his breathing and locked his knees in place because they were actually shaking. "A story my mom told me right before she died about my great-great-great-great-grandmother, who was actually a slave."

Kerris blinked several times, processing the surprising information.

"I know it's hard to believe looking at me, but she was an eighth black." He studied her face with a wry smile. "People were probably always trying to figure out what she was, too. I guess you know what that's like."

Kerris looked away, but a small smile tugged at the soft line of her mouth.

"She was the master's mistress." Walsh grimaced before continuing. "She had two of his children. Those are my ancestors. But the story my mother told was about Great-Grandma Maddie and Asher, not her and the master."

"Asher?" Kerris looked up at Walsh, frowning. "Who was he?"

"He was a slave on the plantation, and he fell in love with her almost instantly. He loved her, but he couldn't live that way. Said he'd rather die than watch her with another man for the rest of his life. So he ran away. Escaped, but had to leave her behind."

Walsh pressed on with the story, hoping it would make as much sense to her as it had to him.

"He went on to fight for the Union, and when the war was over, he returned to North Carolina to find Maddie. The master had died in the war, but had left her, as a free woman, a plot of land and a small bit of money to raise his two children with. That land and that little bit of money was the foundation for my family's success.

"When Asher found her, she was raising the master's kids and working that land by herself. He married her. He didn't care that she'd been the master's mistress, or that she'd had the master's children, or that she was living on land the master had left her. He just knew she was his soul mate, and he'd do whatever it took to spend the rest of his life with her. They took their second chance."

"Walsh, that's beautiful." Kerris curled her hand into a fist on his chest, her eyes telling him the story had landed with her the same way it had for him.

"Yeah, it is." Walsh smiled for the first time since he had started. "My mom told me that story because I asked if she believed in soul mates. I thought I had found and lost mine."

Walsh saw the tears standing in Kerris's eyes and felt the band restricting his chest loosen inch by inch. He pulled a small ring from his pocket. It was a simple gold band. Not flashy, or expensive, but with an intricate pattern etched into the surface. His mother left her original wedding band for her father, but this one—this one she'd left for Walsh.

"Mom said I came from a long line of romantics, and she knew that I would find a way to love. That's why she left me this when she died. It's the ring Asher gave my great-grandma Maddie."

Walsh stooped several inches until they were almost eye level. He searched her eyes and saw the answer before he asked the question. His heart banged against his chest like it wanted out so it could fall at her feet.

"Kerris, will you please, please marry me?" He plowed on, almost afraid to give her the chance to refuse. "I know you just got divorced today, and it might look bad, but I can't live another day without this promise. I want to wake up yours every day for the rest of my life. And I have to know you're mine. It doesn't have to be this ring. Good grief, I could go to Harry Winston or—"

"Don't you dare."

Kerris reached for the hand holding the simple gold band. She looked at him, and he'd never seen her eyes so sure. So confident. So certain. He didn't know if his love had done that for her, or if she had done it for herself, but it was the most beautiful thing he'd ever witnessed.

"I don't actually care how it looks." She watched him through her lashes, coquettish for once. "If you're sure you want me…"

"Kerris, I've never been more sure of anything in my life." He hated the tears he had to blink away. He wanted to get through this without wussing out. "You are the soul mate I thought I'd never get to live my life with. I'm pinching myself that we get a second chance. Please don't make me wait any longer, baby."

"I…well, if you want…yes, I'll marry you."

Walsh scooped her up, his forearms under her bottom, pulled her off the ground, and rested his forehead against hers, not even ashamed that the tears rebelled and charged down his face. He was holding every dream that mattered right here in his arms. His greatest ambition was to love her, to spoil her, to give her the family she'd always wanted.

Even though it had been a hard road, a messy road, littered with the potholes of their mistakes, Walsh embraced that journey. He wasn't sure he would have fully appreciated how much it meant to have Kerris had he not lost her. He gripped her like she might disappear, easing up when she laughed and said she couldn't breathe. Now that they finally had each other, he promised himself he'd never let go.

Chapter Twenty-Five

I think you're even more beautiful the second time around, Kerris."

Kerris met Meredith's eyes in the mirror before studying her own reflection. Her dark hair spilled around her shoulders, free and waving. She wore no veil, which she thought was fitting because this time, she had nothing to hide. Her mouth was tinted pale rose and stretched into a smile she couldn't hold back no matter how hard she tried. The glints of gold in her amber-colored eyes reflected the gold embroidery piping the startling white of her dress.

"I can't get over this." Jo ran reverent fingers over the material skimming Kerris's slim shape. "I couldn't have chosen better. Vera Wang couldn't have done better. No designer could have."

"I couldn't have either." Kerris touched the orchid charm dangling at her neck. "I love that Walsh chose it for me."

Cam may not be attending their wedding, but he had given her the best wedding present possible. After he'd gone, she'd found what he left for her in the office—the dress Walsh had brought back from Kenya so long ago. Cam had hidden it from her then. He had hidden a lot from her before, and she had hidden so much from herself and those she loved. But not today.

The African gown fell to her feet, pristine and shot with gold threads. She couldn't wait for Walsh to see it. It would be the only surprise, since they had chosen each detail of this day together. Her first wedding had been to the wrong man with two hundred wedding guests looking on. She'd carried calla lilies she didn't like, and a lump of dread and anxiety had sat like coal in her belly all day. Today, there was such peace, and as much as the tabloids would love to intrude, they had no idea. This simple ceremony would take place at a covered bridge suspended over the river with only a few sworn-to-secrecy family and friends present. She was a mere month removed from her divorce. They might still cause a scandal once word got out, but Kerris had reached that place of complete indifference to any opinion except Walsh's.

"Okay, so you have something new." Meredith gestured to the diamond earrings designed to look like feathers, a gift from Walsh that Kerris liked to think of as bohemian luxury. "And you have something borrowed."

Kerris had been shocked when Martin Bennett offered a trio of gorgeous pearl-studded bangles as her something borrowed. Kristeene had admired them once and Martin had gotten them for her, but they had divorced before he had the chance to give them to her. Kerris was humbled by his thoughtfulness. He and Walsh had come so far in the last few years, and his excitement about the wedding had been the greatest proof of that.

"I wanted to cover something blue, if you don't have anything." Jo extended a satin bag with a silky ribbon tied around its neck.

Kerris opened the bag and pulled out a powder blue garter of lace and satin, light as a cobweb in her hand.

"The women in our family have worn this on their wedding day for generations." Jo swallowed and blinked a few times before controlling the emotion her face almost expressed. "Aunt Kris eloped and never got to, but I know she'd want you to have it to-day."

Jo knelt on the floor and carefully pulled the soft material of Kerris's dress up from the hem. Kerris slid the garter up her thigh, smiling at the image of Jo, so regal even on her knees. Jo caught her eyes and offered a smile.

"I don't have to ask this time if you love him," Jo said, standing to her feet. "I know you do, and I know you'll take care of him for me."

"I can't wait to give this garter back to you, Jo, on your wedding day."

Jo's laugh was a rough bark, so at odds with her refined appearance—hair caught at the back of her neck in an elegant bundle and gorgeous rose-colored silk dress draped around her lean body.

"That might take a miracle at this point."

Kerris smiled, thinking of the implausible road that had led her to this day. That had led her to the man waiting just beyond the docked houseboat where she was getting dressed. Who even now stood under a covered bridge waiting to start the rest of their lives together. It had taken no less than a series of miracles to unite them.

"Lucky for you," Kerris said to Jo as she headed toward the door, "I still believe in those."

What else but a miracle would find her standing in front of Walsh Bennett moments later? His rakish grin deepened when Mama Jess handed her over to him. There was so little that was conventional about this day, so Mama Jess giving her away made complete sense. She gave Walsh one of her stern looks, but the tears in her eyes spoiled the effect. Meredith stood as Kerris's maid of honor, her hair, pink as cotton candy, bright and glaring in the September sun. Walsh stood alone, no best man, and even as Kerris walked across the scattering of orchid petals to reach him, she wondered about Cam. He wasn't here today, but she believed in her heart that he would be back in their lives when the time was right for them all.

Soon, there was no room for anyone else except the man facing her, smiling at her like they were all alone. As it often did, the world narrowed down to this one man who had breathed life into places she'd thought long dead. The one who had given "forever" meaning. Enduring love burned in the eyes he fixed on her. He ran his hand down the sleeve of the dress he hadn't seen in so long and had never expected to see again. For a second pain flashed through the joy in his eyes, and Kerris knew he recognized Cam's gift to them. That was their journey, though. Joy, spiked with pain. They had walked through fire to reach each other, and these final moments, though singed, were absolutely perfect because they had found a way to share the rest of their lives.

The minister invited them to say the vows they had written for each other. As Walsh said each word, they fell on her heart like a final balm, healing hurts she had once thought beyond repair.

"This I vow with all the love my heart can hold. I will never leave you. I'll love you without condition. I'll love you when times are hard, and I'll relish all the good days ahead. I will love you until my final breath. Loving you is my greatest privilege. My heart fought to find you, and now that we have each other, I will never let go. I will love you always."

And after all they had endured, after all he had sacrificed to love and have her, Kerris knew that he would.

Epilogue

About a Year Later...

Kerris was having that dream again. The one where Walsh traversed the lines of her body, skimming across the subtle curves with his hands. His wicked fingers kneaded her breasts, and he worshipped her dips and crevices with his mouth. His palms caressed the skin of her inner thighs, working their way toward the pulsing center of her body.

The slide of skin against skin teased her from the murky half consciousness of sleep. Walsh pressed her knees back, capturing her eyes with his and opening her like a flower to him. Such a sweet invasion, a push into her soul. Her body clung to him, begrudging him every withdrawal. Welcoming every thrust.

Walsh laced his fingers with hers and pushed their hands above their heads, dropping his head beside hers on the pillow, lavishing kisses down her cheeks, leaving breath-wrapped words in her ear.

"Baby, you're everything."

Kerris arched up, luring him deeper into her body until there wasn't even room for light or sound between them. Joined at the center. Joined at the heart. A fusion of flesh and soul. It was too much, a chaos of irresistible sensation reducing her to the basest response. Gasps. Grunts. Tears watering their kisses. Walsh licked into the corners of her mouth. He dragged one hand over the slope of her shoulder and the curve of her waist and gripped her thigh.

"Oh, God, Walsh, it hurts to love like this. So sweet it hurts."

Like a sugar-tipped shard of glass piercing her heart. Every time.

His words, his love, stole her breath and her thoughts until there was nothing but her body offering him everything. Nothing but shudders and screams and the cries he swallowed and the love they made. She captured her bottom lip between her teeth, eyes clenched, nails digging into his shoulders.

It was like swimming into a violent current, beautifully imperiled, but perfectly safe. They shared tremors. They shuddered and trembled against each other until they both lay still. Until they both lay sated.

"Good morning." Walsh grinned, kissing her collarbone. "Merry Christmas."

"Was that my first Christmas present?" Kerris asked, voice husky and hoarse with pleasure.

"First? Greedy woman, after that, you shouldn't need anything else."

She laughed the full-throated laugh she saved for these intimate times, saved for him.

"I know you too well, Walsh Bennett, to think early-morning sex is the only thing I'll be getting from you for Christmas. I'd be fine with that, though. It was pretty incredible."

"I aim to please. You're right, though. There are other gifts. I am determined to spoil you even if we have to come to blows over it."

"Doesn't that kind of defeat the purpose?" She laughed, reaching up to dig her fingers into the dark hair curling at his neck.

"Not if coming to blows means I get to spank you."

She rose, pulling herself up to straddle him. She clutched the sheet around her shoulders against the chilly morning air for a moment before letting it drop and grinning when his eyes crawled over her nakedness.

"Yes, please."

"Baby, you know what it does to me when you say please."

She did. Her second Christmas gift was very much like the first.

An hour later, Kerris tightened the belt on her kimono, grinning at her reflection in the mirror, her amber eyes glinting with anticipation.

"Walsh!" She raised her voice to be heard over the shower, jumping up onto the marbled countertop, pressing her back to the mirror and allowing her feet to dangle over the side.

"Huh?" He turned off the shower and stepped out to drape a fluffy towel around his hips. "What's up, baby?"

"I know we said we'd exchange gifts when everyone else got here." She bit her lip to hide a secret smile. "But I have one gift I want to give you alone. Just us."

"Is this better than the gift you just gave me in the shower?" He slanted her a wicked, reminiscent smile. Leaning against the counter, he tugged on one of her toes.

"Um, yeah," she said, amazed she could still blush after the last year with this sensual creature she'd married.

She reached into the bathroom counter drawer, pulling out a

black box with a silver bow. She proffered it with a shy smile. He leaned forward to take it, kissing her with gentle hunger, still holding the waiting gift.

"Walsh," she said against his searching mouth. "We'll never be ready for our guests if you don't stop and open your gift."

"It's just our family." He pulled her bottom lip between his teeth, his hand cupping her breast and plucking at her nipple.

Her body didn't care that they'd had sex twice this morning. Heat flooded the center of her as she pressed into the fingers sliding down her waist, between her legs.

Oh, God, focus.

"Walsh, we can't."

"They'll understand, baby. We're newlyweds."

Kerris slid down the counter, putting a few inches between them.

"That's what you said the last time we invited your father over for dinner. He was expecting a home-cooked meal and ended up with sandwiches. Not to mention, he *heard* us up here. I was mortified."

Walsh barked a quick laugh. "That's what he gets for using his old key."

"That won't happen today. Everything will be ready and on the table when they arrive. Now open the gift."

"Okay, okay." Walsh slid up onto the counter beside her, carefully removing the silver bow. Inside was a clear plastic case. And inside the clear plastic case was...

"This is a pregnancy test." He sketched a frown with his dark brows.

"Wow, you're as smart as they say you are."

"And there're two lines. That means..."

"That means the world better watch out, because Walsh Bennett has procreated." She laughed, unable to contain the joy spilling from her eyes and the smile she refused to hold back any longer.

Walsh jerked Kerris over onto his lap, crushing her against him. He rocked her back and forth, eyes closed, head buried in her hair.

"Walsh?" Kerris faltered a little. "I thought you'd be jumping around and screaming from the rooftop. Are you not...are you okay with it?"

"Yeah," he said, his voice husky with emotion. He blinked away tears. "Sorry, I'm such a wuss. I just didn't think I could be any happier."

She leaned away from him, studying the moisture in his eyes with a small smile. She reached up to cup his firm, still-stubbled jaw, forcing him to look into her eyes.

"Don't worry. I cried, too. I've had some time to get used to it."

"How long have you known? When did you take the test?"

"Last week." She kissed his chin. "It's been hard keeping it from you, but I knew it would be the perfect Christmas gift, so I saved it."

"Kerris, we haven't been married long. Are you sure you're okay with it? I don't want you to feel pressured—"

"Walsh, I couldn't be happier."

"Me either," he said without hesitation. His proud grin faltered, concern still in his eyes when he looked at her. "Are you okay about...I mean, Amalie."

Even now her baby girl's name pricked Kerris's heart, though less each day. Amalie would always be her first child. She might always mourn her in small ways on unexpected days, but this joy sat right alongside that pain as a comfort; as a reminder of life moving forward and getting better.

"I will never forget her, but I look at it like this." Kerris touched her stomach, a smile dawning slowly on her face. "Our kids are lucky because they'll have a big sister up there looking after them their whole lives."

Walsh leaned in and dropped a kiss on the one tear that slipped down her cheek and watered her smile.

"That's right, baby. They will."

They sat there on the counter, dreaming about the little life already growing inside of her, punctuating the hollow silence in the bathroom with husky laughs and whispers. Kerris allowed them to bask in the glow for as long as she could before she reminded him that she still had work to do. Kerris hastily dressed so she could head downstairs. She shook her head, smiling at Walsh sitting on the bed, one pant leg on, one off, staring down at the two stripes declaring him a daddy.

* * *

"Walsh, stay out of that stuffing." Kerris opened the oven to check the turkey, flashing him a mock frown.

"You know what they say about idle hands." Walsh pressed his chest to her back, sandwiching her between his body and the stove.

"Could these hands"—Kerris turned around and shifted his hands from her hips—"set the table for me? Everyone'll be here soon, and I still have a few things to do."

"When will we get some help around here? You know, a maid, a cook."

"You're looking at 'em, buddy." She sampled the broth boiling on the stovetop, offering him an impish grin. "I want to do things for us for as long as I can. I want to make this a home and take care of you. I don't need someone else doing it."

"Kerris," he said, his face sobering. "I'm serious. Especially, now that you're pregnant, I don't want you handling things by yourself."

"What else will I do?"

"Well, between the work you've started doing with the foundation, the Riverstone Collection, and running Déjà Vu long distance—"

"I would hardly call scouring the city every once in a while for stuff I can send back to Rivermont 'running' Déjà Vu." Kerris popped a sweet potato pie in the oven. "Thank God Mer has help now. I feel so guilty sometimes leaving her and Mama Jess handling everything without me."

"We'll have to postpone that trip to Kenya." Walsh looked over his shoulder from the dining room. He pulled the china from the hutch.

"Walsh, no." Kerris stepped out of the kitchen and into the dining room, frowning and wiping her hands on a dishtowel. "Pregnant women can travel all the way up to the last trimester."

"Not my pregnant woman, not to Kenya." Walsh's tone brooked no argument. "There'll be plenty of time later."

"I enjoyed our trip this summer so much," she said. "We can squeeze in a quick trip in the next couple of months."

"Ker, no," he said, quiet and firm, not looking up from the place settings he was laying down.

"Walsh, but I—"

"No, babe."

Kerris recognized his boardroom stare, and hoped he didn't think she was fooled. She knew he couldn't deny her anything she ever wanted, even though she never abused the fact.

She smiled with gamine persuasion, moving to answer the doorbell.

"We'll talk about it later."

"We will not—" Walsh cut himself off, shaking his head and smiling.

Kerris could already tell this pregnancy would be a tug of war between them. Her always wanting to press the limits, and him determined she'd get nowhere near the edge of them.

"Kerris!" Jo gave Kerris a tight hug and a kiss on the cheek before pulling back so they could give each other once-overs.

"Jo, you look amazing."

And she did. Jo's trademark chestnut angled bob had grown longer, the ends hanging like silk around her shoulders. Her model's body seemed even fitter than the last time Kerris saw her. Her skin, smooth and creamy, glowed from the winter cold. Kerris didn't know which designer had made the chocolate-colored leather dress Jo was wearing, but it seemed to have been sewn along the curves of her body like a layer of expensive skin.

"Jo, what I wouldn't give to have a butt like that." Kerris gave her own slim-for-now curves a quick glance.

Jo looked over her shoulder as if to check and make sure the junk was still beautifully in the trunk.

"We all get a little something." Jo laughed, patting her own ass. "Or in my case, not so little. You look great, as always. New York is treating you fine."

"I'm treating her fine." Walsh strode into the foyer to hug Jo, too. "How's it going, cuz?"

"Where's Mama Jess?" Kerris looked back out into the street behind Jo.

Kerris saw Meredith and Mama Jess climbing the short flight of stairs up to their door, with Uncle James pulling up the rear. She had been ecstatic when they agreed to come to New York for Christmas. They were all staying with them in the town house for the next week, and Kerris could barely contain her excitement.

She was happiest of all when Martin Bennett arrived, gift bags in hand. Walsh hugged him. To see his father sitting at their table for Christmas dinner, laughing and at ease with the people who meant the most to them, swelled Kerris's heart. The tenuous bond the two men had forged since Kristeene's death had continued to deepen. Kristeene would be pleased.

They dug into dinner, the whole house humming with the sounds of cheerful reunion and Kerris's holiday playlist. There were hugs all around with everyone dragging gifts out from under the huge tree Kerris had insisted on. They exchanged gifts with one another, bathed in the glow of the fire Walsh had lit. The peal of the doorbell barely carried over the buzz of their merriment and conversation.

"Could you get that, Jo?" Walsh leaned back on the couch with his arm around Kerris's shoulder. "I'm too stuffed to move."

"Lazy boy, you weren't too stuffed to go back for your third helping five minutes ago." Jo opened the door, and her mouth fell open when she saw who was on the doorstep. "Cam!"

Kerris stiffened in Walsh's arms.

"Hey, sweetie." Cam's deep voice rumbled into the room. He pulled Jo off her feet and whirled her around twice. "It's been forever. You look…damn, you look good, Jo."

Kerris watched Jo lift her hand to her hair, smiling uncertainly into the sharp masculine beauty of Cam's face.

"He knows I'm coming." Cam grinned, reading the question on Jo's face. "You don't have to run for cover."

Walsh walked into the foyer as if Cam showed up on their doorstep every day.

"I was hoping you'd actually show your ass up." He extended his hand to Cam.

"When have I ever turned down food?" Cam offered his hand, but kept the guard over his smile.

Kerris glanced between the two men she loved so much and so differently. They seemed to be watching each other with wary gladness. Maybe they were ready to try.

"Did we move the party out here or something?" Kerris walked to the foyer, wading into the conversation. She shot a quick, exploratory glance her husband's way, returning his slow smile with one of her own.

"This is another Christmas gift for you." Walsh grabbed her hand and walked with her, pushing her in Cam's direction, watching their quick, awkward hug.

"Cam?" She looked up at her ex-husband, once Walsh's best friend. She wasn't sure what he was to them now, or who had reached out to whom, but she sensed a definite shift since the last time they'd been in the same room together.

"We've kind of been talking a little." Cam slid one hand into the pocket of his black leather sports coat.

"A couple of times by phone," Walsh chimed in, reaching for Kerris's hand. "At first, more for the promise my mom had you make than anything else."

"Yeah." Cam's smile slipped a little. "Speaking of which, I left something in the car. Be right back."

He dashed back out the door and down the steps. Kerris turned to Walsh, raising her brows before she voiced the question.

"Are you okay?"

"Hey, I don't know if it'll ever be the same between us," Walsh admitted with a rueful smile. "It's still a little awkward. How could it not be? But we both want to try. Are *you* okay with it?"

"Walsh, this is the best gift you could've given me." She twined her arms around his waist and laid her head against his chest.

When Cam came back through the door, she jerked her head up, stepping away.

"It's okay, Kerris." Cam laughed, his eyes more serious than his smile. "I do know you guys are married now. We have a lot to put behind us, but it's behind us. Okay?"

"Okay." She split a smile between the two men who had been the most special in her life. "Then I want my gift."

Cam waved her back into the living room, where Jo had returned and the others were waiting. Jo had obviously apprised Martin and Mama Jess of the situation because they all watched the three of them coming through the door with varying degrees of skepticism and fascination.

"Hey, everybody," Cam greeted casually, as if he hadn't been the eye of the three-way storm he, Kerris, and Walsh had lived through over the last few years. Everyone greeted him easily enough, eyeing him with guarded hospitality.

"Well, ain't you a sight," Mama Jess said, crossing her hands over her midriff and her feet at the ankles. "They ain't got barbers in Paris?"

Cam ran one hand through the dark hair hanging around his neck, giving her the smile that had never met a woman it couldn't charm.

"He probably thinks it adds to his artist allure now that he's gotten a taste of the big-time," Walsh said.

Cam looked uncomfortable for a minute before rolling his eyes and rocking back on the heels of his black Italian leather boots. Paris must be treating him well.

"Yeah, that's it, Bennett," Cam said, coating the words in sarcasm.

"Did I miss something?" Martin asked. "You're famous now, Cam?"

"No, sir." Cam took off his coat and folded it over his arm.

"He's being modest, Uncle Martin." Jo linked her arm with Cam's, leaning into his shoulder. "Someone made a documentary about Cam's graffiti art in Paris and it won at Sundance."

"I was just in the right place at the right time." Cam tugged Jo's hair and smiled at her wince. "Holding a can of spray paint."

"And the two music videos that just featured your paintings?" Jo demanded, her face wearing a proud smile. "Was that a fluke?"

"Maybe not," Cam said, giving her a fond shake. "You should keep all the sketches I've ever given you. They might be worth something some day."

"I have every one of them." Jo bit her lip and looked like she wanted to gobble the telling words back up.

Cam watched Jo an extra second before smiling and dropping a quick kiss on her hair, speaking before the silence grew awkward.

"Speaking of keeping my sketches, I have a little something for Walsh and Kerris."

He presented the large square he'd brought back inside with him to Walsh before settling down on the couch beside Jo, draping her shoulder with his arm. Walsh carefully pulled away the brown paper shrouding the gift. He peered down at the canvas in his hands. He looked up at Cam's somber face. Kerris saw Walsh swallow, gulping back the emotion she knew he had to be fighting. He slowly turned it around so that everyone could see.

Kerris's breath caught at the beauty of it. It was Kristeene. The rich colors of the painting had been skillfully muted so that the most vibrant, most alive, most striking thing in the entire painting was her eyes. They were lit with the otherworldly gleam Kerris had noticed in her last days: a look of hard-won peace that only those facing death's inevitable call could acquire. It was that resigned contentment, that gritty grace she'd gained in her horrific battle with cancer, but set in the face Kerris remembered when she'd first met her. Smooth and unlined by pain. Laughing, the regal bones pronounced against the smooth skin.

Kerris turned her head in the direction of a choked sound, astounded to see Martin Bennett struggling to his feet and walking over to stand beside Walsh, his fingers trembling as he traced the artful strokes of the painting.

"I sketched her that last day at the hospital before she went home for good," Cam said, returning the squeeze Jo consoled his hand with.

"It's magnificent," Walsh breathed, blinking back tears. "You captured her perfectly, man. I can't thank you enough."

Kerris's eyes locked with Cam's in perfect understanding. This was as close to a blessing as they'd ever get from him. She mouthed "thank you," smiling when his olive skin reddened and he inclined his head, acknowledging her gratitude.

"I have the sketch." Cam rose from the couch and reached into his back pocket. He pulled out a folded sheet of sketch paper, extending it to Martin. "Been carrying this around for a long time."

Martin fixed his eyes on the likeness Cam had sketched in charcoal, firming his lips into a straight line.

"You can have it," Cam offered with a half-smile to Walsh's father.

"Thank you," Martin said, his voice heavy with barely checked emotion.

Kerris glanced over at Meredith and Mama Jess, the only family she'd had for a long time, their loyalty the only thing she'd been able to count on during her long year of recovery. Somehow, miraculously, she had found Mama Jess again, and their bond had survived the worst circumstances and years of living apart.

Then there was Jo and Cam, now huddled on the couch, teasing and tickling each other, falling into their friendly intimacy like a habit they could never break. Blocking out the rest of the world like they often did. Tuning into each other and tuning out everything else. Kerris's heart lifted with possibility for them. Maybe finally…maybe one day…maybe soon.

And then Kerris's eyes fell on Walsh, who chose that moment to look up from the painting he still held and into her eyes. The same thread that had always stretched between them pulled strong, invisible, unbreakable. She saw her future in those eyes. The children she'd longed for; the family she'd coveted. As a little girl, she had prayed for a home, and he was that. He was her country. His heart was her homeland.

And he and Cam were in the same room, not snarling at each other, but forging new bonds of friendship, repairing the old.

Kristeene Bennett's face stared back at her from the heavy canvas, and Kerris felt a weight lift under those resolved eyes. Did she know that Kerris had kept her promise? Was she watching them even now? Did Kristeene gain a measure of peace from their reconciliation? And then Kerris understood. The promise had not been for Kristeene's peace of mind, but for theirs. Kerris touched her stomach, a smile playing across her mouth. Their future was growing inside of her, and she could face it with the clear heart of a promise kept.

Turn the page for a preview of
the next book in the Bennett series

Be Mine Forever

Coming February 2015!

No one could ever accuse Cam Mitchell's eyes of being just blue or just gray. They were instead a mesmerizing intercourse of the two colors. A gorgeous, God-spun mixture of sea and clouds. At least that's how Jo Walsh had always thought of them. She couldn't see them right now with Cam's forehead pressed to the viewing window.

Watching him unobserved for a moment was a privilege. The dark hair, always unruly, fell around his neck, undecided about whether to wave or curl. The broad shoulders pushed forward and his hands burrowed into the pockets of the jeans it had taken this long to look that good. He banged his head against the window, lightly enough that the babies on the other side wouldn't be disturbed. But maybe just hard enough to hurt a little.

The *clack-clack* of her four-inch Manolos brought Cam's head swiveling in her direction. Jo drew in the bracing breath she always needed at the first sight of him after a long time. She kept thinking, kept hoping that one day Cam wouldn't affect her this way. That her heart wouldn't seize with disbelief that any man could be this beautiful in real life. That all the steel-reinforced walls she'd erected wouldn't topple when that blazing white smile flashed at her like lighting. She was never fully prepared for that smile, always a bolt to her unsuspecting system.

Only there was no smile tonight.

Sadness cloaked and slumped Cam's shoulders and turned down the corners of his mouth. He offered her those one-of-a-kind eyes for a few moments before considering the babies again without saying a word.

Jo slid damp palms across the soft material clinging to her hips. She had just gotten back to the office after a fund-raising luncheon when Cam called. She still wore the Kelly green dress outlining her every asset. Convenient. She hadn't had time to think about what she would wear or how she would style her hair or any of the nonsense she typically considered when she knew she'd see Cam.

A lot of good it ever did her.

She stepped into the space beside him, turning her head to consider his rugged profile.

"You doing okay?" Jo pressed the tips of her fingers to the glass separating them from the infants.

"You mean since we last talked, or since I had to stand in for Walsh with Kerris in the delivery room?"

Jo caught the wince before it made it to her face, but inside she ached for Cam. He'd fled to Paris after Amalie's death. Stayed there while Walsh wooed Kerris. He had done so well for himself away from them, but she'd always known he'd be back. The thing Cam wanted more than anything in the world had been a family.

With Aunt Kris gone, Jo, Walsh, even Kerris—they might be the closest he'd ever come. But to be drawn into the pulsing center of Kerris and Walsh's new life together had to be hard. Had to resurrect feelings he might have thought settled.

"I'm sorry it happened like that, Cam."

He finally looked away from his boots and the babies long enough to offer her one of those smiles that, without any real effort, punched a hole in her chest where her heart used to be before Cam stole it over fifteen years ago. Some days, she didn't think she'd ever get it back. She didn't really have much use for it anyway.

"It's fine." Cam drew his dark brows into a quick frown. "I mean, it's shit, but it's fine. *I'm* fine. How's Kerris and the girls?"

Even Jo couldn't govern the joy that pressed its way past her impassive expression.

"Kerris is fine. The girls are gorgeous. In ICU, of course, but that's pretty standard for preemies."

"Names?"

"Brooklin and Harlim." Jo snorted. "We're lucky it's not Apple and Orange, I guess."

Cam added a grin to the knowing look he slid over to her. They had always teased Walsh about his "high life" in the city. Jo might never miss Fashion Week in New York, and she might make regular shopping pilgrimages to Paris, but to her Rivermont was home. Had always been. Would always be.

"How is Walsh?" Cam's mouth dropped the smile it had managed to hold on to for a few seconds.

"As you would expect, going crazy because he can't get here at the speed of light. Probably making everyone in a twenty-mile radius miserable."

"That sounds right." Cam turned to face her, shoulder to the glass. "I didn't want to see them. The twins, I mean. Even now, I can't see them. I don't know when I'll be able to."

Jo ran a steady hand through the hair hanging around her shoulders so she wouldn't reach for him.

"I know seeing Walsh and Kerris—"

"It's not Walsh and Kerris." Cam raised a thick fan of lashes to look at her, eyes unshielded. "What if the twins look like Amalie?"

The thought hadn't even occurred to Jo. Of course, they could look like Amalie, the daughter Kerris and Cam had lost. Brooklin and Harlim shared half the DNA Amalie had died with.

"I'm so sorry, Cam." What else was there to say?

"It's like every time I think I can get past this…debacle between the three of us, and I can maybe be in their lives on some terms, something pushes me back out. Maybe I'm just meant to be…"

Alone.

He didn't say it, but Jo had always known, even when Cam would vacation with them, sleep over at the house, laugh and even cry with them, that some part of him was always alone. Even she, closer to him than anyone else, knew there were places in Cam's life and in his heart not even she could go.

"They want you in their lives," Jo said, feeling like an idiot for saying it, but knowing it was true.

"Yeah, well, we'll see. Some things just aren't worth the hurt." Cam whooshed air from his chest and pulled his lips into that smile he used to change the subject. "So, you staying here or what?"

"No, Kerris is asleep, resting. The nurses are with the girls. Mama Jess and Meredith just got here, actually. They're with Kerris." Jo glanced at the ALOR watch circling her wrist. "I'm done.

Been in constant motion since four o'clock this morning. I'll come back tomorrow."

"Where are you staying?"

"Walsh said I could stay at their place, of course."

"By yourself? Or you could stay with me. We could catch up."

Jo raised an imperious eyebrow and cocked her head to the side.

"Oh, so now you want to catch up. Where have you been for the last six months? Why have you been ignoring me?"

"Jo, I've been busy."

"Don't do that." Some hybrid of a sigh and a laugh slipped past her lips. "Not to me."

He looked at her, his eyes hiding more from her than usual, before they dropped and slid down the length of her body, pausing at her breasts, caressing the line of her waist. She felt that look like a hand skimming over her and shuddered at even the thought of Cam's intimate touch. Something heated up between them, fogging her judgment. It felt like attraction. Felt like chemistry. Felt like something she had hoped for before with Cam, but knew she'd never have.

Jo shook off the effects of that look, wondering if she was going a little crazy. Maybe her feverish mind, always hot and usually bothered around Cam, had conjured that moment. It wouldn't be the first time she read too much into a look or a feeling with this man. For example, at Christmas, she had sensed...she had thought...she had hoped...but nothing had materialized. Cam had gone dark, and she hadn't heard from him until today.

She was just about to clear her throat, but he beat her to it.

"I'm staying at the Chevalier."

Wow. Jo knew between the inheritance Aunt Kris had left him and the money his art had generated the last year or so he had to be sitting pretty, but hearing he was staying at the Chevalier still surprised her. People like Walsh wore wealth. Not as clothing, but as skin. As scent. It had been woven into the fibers of who they were since birth. Walsh could walk into a room naked and you'd assume he came from money. It was in his bearing. In the way he looked at the world like he owned most of it because in some ways, he did. Jo knew this because she was the same.

Even though Jo, with her trained eye, recognized the fine Italian leather of the boots hiding under Cam's weathered jeans, she knew Cam didn't carry wealth the way she and Walsh did. He never seemed uneasy with it. More like he'd simply added it to all the other baggage he was carting around.

"The Chevalier, huh?" Jo turned down the corners of her mouth and offered a ladylike grunt. "I'm impressed."

"Don't be. A, uh…friend has a suite there, and she's letting me crash."

That was more like it. The sizzling moment she had imagined with Cam moments before fizzled into nothing. She'd watched a parade of women march through Cam's life for more than a decade. Not shocking that some woman was so enamored she'd offer him a suite at one of the most luxurious hotels in the world.

"You sure it's okay for me to stay?"

"Yeah, of course. She's in Paris." Cam pushed away from the glass and linked his arm through Jo's and started toward the elevators. "She's not coming to the States until next week and wouldn't mind anyway. There's two bedrooms in the suite."

"I'll just call Pierce, Uncle Martin's driver." Jo pulled her phone from her Bottega Veneta hobo. "He picked me up and has my bags. We can bum a ride to the hotel if you want."

"Sounds great." Cam glanced once more over his shoulder at

the infants through the glass. "I need a drink. I didn't see my day turning out like this."

Seeing Cam after he'd ignored her for the last six months. Witnessing Walsh's twin girls come into the world. The day had held more than one surprise. And she couldn't prove it, but she felt like there might be more to come.

About the Author

There were several signs that Kennedy Ryan would be a writer, but making up stories with a mop as her long-haired heroine while the other kids played kick ball may have been the most telling. After graduating with her journalism degree from UNC–Chapel Hill (GO, HEELS!), she found various means of gainful employment having absolutely nothing to do with said degree, but knew she would circle back to writing, in some form or fashion. After years of working and writing for nonprofit organizations, she finally returned to her first love—telling stories.

In an alternative universe and under her government name, Tina Dula, she is wife to Sam, mom to Myles, and a friend to those living with autism. A portion of her royalties will go toward her foundation, Myles-A-Part, serving Georgia families, and to her national charitable partner, Talk About Curing Autism (TACA).

You can learn more at:
KennedyRyanWrites.com
Twitter: @KennedyRWrites
Facebook.com

CPSIA information can be obtained at www.ICGtesting.com
Printed in the USA
LVOW08s1021101014

408210LV00001B/17/P